EXODUS

THE BELT BOOK FIVE

GERALD M. KILBY

OUTER PLANET
MEDIA

For notifications on promotions and updates for upcoming books,
please join my Readers Group at www.geraldmkilby.com.

You will also find a link to download my techno-thriller REACTION
and the follow-up novella EXTRACTION for FREE.

AN AVATRON AWAKENS

long row of remote-controlled robot avatars, known as avatrons, stood mute and inert in their docking stations in the administrative sector of New World One, the vast orbital habitat that had been constructed out in the asteroid belt.

Ever since the destruction of the quantum intelligence on Ceres and the subsequent attack on the New World by the VanHeilding Corporation, these avatrons had been busy, pressed into service almost daily by a multitude of important people whose input into the administration of the Belt Federation Territories was deemed to be so significant that they required a physical presence at the decision-making table.

Yet an avatron, by its nature, is nothing more than a vessel. A technically very sophisticated one, it must be said, but a vessel nonetheless. Its sole purpose is to provide a physical interface for a remote human operator, enabling them to be on-site, so to speak, even though they both exist in separate locations. In a sense, the avatron becomes the human in robotic form, relaying in real time the actions and voice of the operator, as well as providing visual, audio, and haptic feedback.

But they have their limitations. The primary one being the skill of the operator in utilizing a neural interface, since all actions are *thought* rather than performed. The second is how long it takes for the signal to travel through space. As the distance between avatron and operator increases, so does the reaction time-lag, up to a point where it's simply too long to conduct any meaningful real-time interaction.

Yet as a display panel flickered to life beside one of the fifteen inactive avatrons stored in the council chambers on New World One, the incoming data-stream did not emanate from some local source. It was not some government official down in Rongo City on Ceres, in a hurry to participate in some high-level meeting of the administrative council. Nor was it the CEO of some industrial outpost hoping to negotiate mining rights or finesse profit structures. No, this data-stream was emanating from Mars, over two hundred million kilometers away, and had taken more than fourteen minutes to arrive at the avatron's interface port.

The control panel screen displayed the incoming data-stream in a rainbow of stylized graphics—but only for a moment. It then went dark for a second before bursting back to life, this time displaying a frenetic scrolling stream of code in harsh, utilitarian monochrome.

Had there been a technician present, then perhaps they would have noticed this activation and the subsequent anomaly in the display data. But there were few people around at this time of evening. Even here, on this artificial world, the humans that inhabited it remained creatures of Earth and its solar cycle. They rose to an artificial dawn and wound down as an artificial evening approached. Now it was almost midnight, and few but essential workers and the odd night owl were about. And so the data-stream performed its digital dance with the avatron, unnoticed and unhindered.

After several minutes of constant data input, the screen suddenly went dead. Again, had a technician been monitoring this anomaly then they would have concluded that the process had ended and that the avatron would now come to life, like a marionette balancing on strings of digital data. But it did not. It remained inanimate, tucked away in its high-tech sarcophagus, only for the data-stream to resume some twenty-eight minutes later—the time it took for a signal to be sent back to its source, and for Mars to reply.

This stop-start, send-and-reply transmission continued for many hours until the data-stream finally ceased, the display went blank, and the avatron took its first step out of its docking station.

It shifted its head this way and that, sensing the environment like some forest creature taking a cautious step into an unfamiliar clearing. Satisfied that no threats were imminent, it proceeded to examine its physical self, holding an arm up and turning it around like someone trying on a new coat. This slow, curious robotic tai chi lasted for several more minutes until the avatron was satisfied with its understanding of its physical geometry and functions. It moved cautiously across the storage room and stopped in front of a remote-access terminal. It raised a hand and waved it over the screen. The terminal came to life.

Datagrams flicked across the screen as the avatron searched the New World One data-stack. After a few seconds, it found what it was looking for: the location of Luca Lee-McNabb, the much sought-after granddaughter of Fredrick VanHeilding.

2

DARKNESS AT THE EDGE OF TOWN

I t was late, and Miranda was feeling drained—more so than usual. Yet it was not so much a physical tiredness that affected her; this was a deeper malaise. A fatigue that had taken root in her very being, one wrought by a lifetime of fighting with a family that seemed hellbent on her demise and of those whom she loved.

Luca had still not regained consciousness since her confrontation with the node-runners during the battle for New World One—that was over seven months ago. Now she lay in a hospital bed in intensive care, wired up to a collection of monitors and feeding tubes.

On the upside, she was not brain dead, and according to Dr. Rayman, she was not critical nor in any immediate danger. In reality, she seemed physically fine. Yet that situation would deteriorate over time. The longer she remained catatonic, the more the physical inactivity and the intravenous feeding regime would gnaw away at her physical well-being.

Miranda had been by her side for the last few hours; it was something she did most days. And each time, she would hope that maybe today would be the day that Luca would show some sign of activity, some flicker of an eyelid or twitch of a finger—anything that would indicate a path back to consciousness.

In the beginning, she was so consumed by Luca's welfare that she had taken to sleeping in the hospital. But as time passed and no change seemed imminent, she took up residence elsewhere, and her visits became shorter—once or twice she would even skip a day. Yet this ritual still took up most of her time—what else did she have to do?

Scott would also visit nearly every day, and with no response from Luca, the only thing left for them to do was to talk. This was just small talk at first, but soon they would plumb the depths of their mutual past, both trying to understand what had happened to them, and how it had come to this.

FINISHED with her visit for today, Miranda walked along the wide corridor to the entrance lobby of the hospital and spied Dr. Stephanie Rayman, who had recently started working here.

The doctor acknowledged her with a wave. "You heading off now?" said Steph, coming over.

"Not quite. I was thinking of heading up to the roof terrace, just to gaze at the night for a while." She gestured upward with a pointed finger.

Steph glanced at her slate. "I'll be finished soon. I could follow you up...if that's okay?"

"Of course, always glad of the company."

Steph nodded in reply, and Miranda continued her journey across the lobby to a stairway that led all the way up to the flat roof of the two-story hospital building.

It was a quiet place, usually devoid of people. A place where Miranda liked to go to clear her head. She walked across the open expanse of the roof to a clutch of recliners that someone had the good sense to drag up here. She sat down with a sigh and gazed out across the vast, nighttime vista of the New World One habitat.

Overhead, the sky was ablaze with what looked like a thousand twinkling stars, but these were just the lights from the far side of the giant cylinder—eight kilometers away. Yet in the darkness, it seemed as if the entire habitat was open to the heavens.

Ahead of her, Miranda could see the long lines of the agricultural facilities stretching out along the interior rim. The headlights from the various carts and industrial robots threaded their way along fixed transport routes, like rows of illuminated ants.

To her left, the lights from population clusters increased the closer they got to the end cap, this being the most built-up sector of the habitat. To her right, the scattering of lights began to lessen as the population density thinned out. Farther along, the lights disappeared almost completely into absolute darkness, leaving just a vague impression of the far-off end cap—ten kilometers distant.

"Hey, got something for us."

Miranda glanced around to see Steph standing beside her holding two mugs and what looked like an actual bottle of wine.

"Is that..." She leaned in closer, trying to read the label in the dim light.

Steph handed it to her. "It's supposed to be a genuine bottle of Spanish Rioja...all the way from Earth."

Miranda examined it with a fascinated awe. "Where did you get this? It must be worth a fortune."

"A patient gave it to me. He's one of the Cerellians. You know, the wealthy shipbuilding family. Anyway, he says it's real. Fancy a...mug?" Steph held up one of the utilitarian mycelium mugs that she had brought with her. "These will have to do. I couldn't find anything better in the hospital canteen."

"Are you sure? Don't you want to keep it for a special occasion or something, considering what this must be worth?"

Steph took the bottle from Miranda and proceeded to open it. "It's just a bottle of wine, and besides..."—she gestured at the sprawling nighttime vista—"this is as good a time and place as any."

Miranda took one of the mugs and held it out. "Well then, don't let me stop you—hit me."

Steph filled both mugs, handed one to Miranda, and settled herself down onto a recliner. She raised her mug to Miranda, who reciprocated. "Cheers."

Miranda took a sip. "Oh-my-god. That's amazing."

Steph let out a long, satisfied sigh and gazed out across the habitat landscape. "You know, if it didn't know better, I could be convinced I was back on Earth, sitting out on a warm summer's evening."

Miranda rested her head back on the recliner, a light wind feathering her cheek. "Yeah, I think it's the way the air moves inside the habitat that adds to the illusion." She took another sip of her wine. "How do they do that? Get the air to move like it's a gentle breeze."

"I don't know. I presume they need to keep it circulating... Big fans, I suppose. Feels nice, though. Almost real."

They sat for a while, just soaking up the vista and decompressing from the trials of the day.

Miranda finally broke the silence. "It's staggering to think that humanity can build such a place."

"Yes, it's amazing what we can do when we're not trying to tear ourselves apart." Steph gestured toward the end cap hidden beyond the distant darkness. "Cyrus says that the next five kilometers are almost completed, and they'll be removing the end cap in the next few weeks." She glanced back at Miranda. "This place is going to get a whole lot bigger."

"We're probably going to need it, with the thousands of new people that keep arriving from Ceres."

"It's not just Ceres," said Steph. "I'm seeing a big influx of refugees coming in from the mining regions, out past Vesta. It seems that a small war has broken out now that the QI on Ceres has been destroyed."

Miranda sat up a little and looked over at Steph. "What have you been hearing? How bad is it?"

She took a drink from her mug. "I only know what I've overheard from some people coming through the hospital, but it's bad. Several of the mining corporations see the loss of the QI on Ceres as an opportunity for a land grab. Mainly Xiang Zu Corporation, as far as I can tell."

Miranda sighed. "What the hell is wrong with these people?"

"Human nature, Miranda. Enough is never going to satisfy them. They always want more."

"Yeah, human nature." Miranda gave a shrug and sat back again. "I suppose that's why we need a quantum intelligence network to keep us all in check."

Again, they were silent for a while, each lost in their own thoughts, taking in the dance of the nighttime lights.

"I've decided that it's time for me to leave, head back home to Earth." Steph kept her gaze straight ahead while she dropped this on Miranda.

"Leave?" Miranda sat up again with a jerk, almost spilling her drink.

Steph turned to her with a resigned expression. "Things are getting more unstable here. The violent flare-ups out in the asteroid belt are becoming more frequent. I get the feeling that something big is brewing." She sat up and gave Miranda a hard look. "You need to get out too, as soon as possible, before it all blows up."

Miranda remained quiet for a moment, before raising her mug to Steph. "So this is a kind of going-away party?"

She nodded. "Kind of."

"When are you thinking of departing?"

"In a week or so, as soon as I can organize a flight to Mars, then on to Earth."

"Gonna miss you, Steph. It was great having you around again. I really don't know what we would have done without you."

Steph nodded and raised her mug. "Gonna miss you, too."

They banged their mugs together and took a drink.

"You think Luca will ever come around?" said Miranda after a while.

"I honestly don't know. She's physically fine, normal brain activity, she just...doesn't want to wake up." Steph seemed a little frustrated and started rolling the mug between her hands. "You shouldn't wait, though. You have a ship. Go now, get to Mars where it will be safer. God knows what's going to happen here."

"I know, but I just don't want to risk space travel, all that heavy acceleration. I can't imagine it would be good for Luca. Scott also thinks it would be too risky."

They went quiet again. Some activity had kicked off down at one of the agricultural facilities. Several ground transports had pulled up, ready to load up goods. New people appeared and began milling around, waiting to start the loading.

"How's that going, you and Scott? If you don't mind me asking." Steph said this as she refilled their mugs.

Miranda screwed her mouth up. "Difficult."

"I imagine it can't be easy."

"It isn't, not when my family is trying to kill us all." She looked over at Steph with a smile. "That tends to get a little problematic for a relationship."

"True."

"And it's hard to know what's what after all that's happened these last two decades."

Steph gave her a sympathetic nod.

"Sometimes I get flashes of the old Scott...but mostly I just see the new one." Miranda shrugged. "I don't know why I'm telling you this. Maybe the wine's gone to my head."

"The new one?"

"Distant, more cynical, more world-weary, I suppose."

"I think we're all suffering from a little of that."

"Sure, but it's more than that. I think the age thing gets to him."

"You're both the same age, more or less."

"Steph, look at me. If you didn't know me, what age would you peg me at?"

"Yeah, I get it. You don't age like the rest of us."

"No, I don't. I look like I'm in my late twenties—a legacy of my family's meddling in genetics."

"And I'm supposed to feel sorry for you somehow?"

Miranda gave a long, slow sigh. "I know, why should anyone feel sorry for me? But you need to put yourself in my shoes. I watch on while all those I love grow old around me, and then I'm pushed away as some sort of freak because my presence reminds people of what they've lost. And it's the same fate that awaits Luca—if she ever wakes up."

Steph raised her eyebrows and looked over at her friend. "You shouldn't think that way...because it's simply not true. Yes, I admit I'm a bit envious of your genetics, but you're still Miranda. That hasn't changed. And longevity is not exclusive to you—it's available to anyone...with a few billion in spare cash."

Miranda sighed again. "I suppose you're right. I don't want to sound like a princess, you know... 'Poor me, my arms are so tired from carrying around all this gold.' So don't mind me, I'm just feeling sorry for myself. A lot of stress and uncertainty at the moment."

"That's why you need to get out of here. Go to Mars, where it's safe." Steph poured out the last of the wine. "And don't push Scott away. You're going to need him...in more ways than you think."

Miranda raised her mug. "Thanks Steph, for everything...and especially the wine. I'm going to miss you... Miss your straight-talking."

"Cheers to straight-talking, then." They banged their mugs together.

While Miranda savored her drink—it would be a long time before she tasted anything this fine again—her comms unit pinged a message alert. She tapped the side of her temple to bring it up on her ocular implant. "Speak of the devil. It's Scott." She glanced over at Steph.

"At this hour?" Her words were followed by an alert from her own comms unit. Being old school, she didn't go in for implants, so fished a unit out from a side pocket.

"Crap." Miranda sat bolt upright in the recliner. "He wants to meet right now, says it's urgent."

Steph leaned over and showed Miranda the message on her comms screen.

Miranda glanced at it, then back to Steph. "It's the same message...exactly the same."

"Something's up. We better go."

Miranda stood up, downed her mug, and took a last look at the nighttime landscape. "I hope he's okay."

"Never a dull moment, eh?" Steph gave a wry smile.

3

JUST ANOTHER ROBOT

Having located its target, the avatron disconnected from the access terminal and moved over to the rear wall of the room where a service hatch was located. It placed a hand over the control panel and the hatch swung open to reveal a short metal ladder descending into the service tunnels. These existed between the outer hull of the giant cylinder and the inner floor of the habitat. They spidered their way throughout the entire structure, bringing power and services to all sectors. The avatron stepped in through the open hatch and began climbing down. From here it could get all the way to the hospital complex without fear of detection.

The passageway was low, narrow, and pitch black save for the pinpricks of illumination emanating from the indicator lights of various systems dotted along the side walls. But this offered no difficulty for the avatron since it moved by utilizing its ultrasonic proximity sensors. It had also downloaded a complete schematic of the service tunnels and knew exactly where it was going and how to get there.

But its progress was slow, and it would need to hurry —it didn't have much time. The low, narrow passage hampered its ability to move at speed, so it was almost an hour later when it finally came to another metal ladder leading up to what should be an exit hatch in the power room of the hospital complex.

It started up the ladder and found the hatch slightly open. Someone may have been using it; the avatron needed to be careful. It raised its head slowly above the lower rim of the hatch, placed a hand on the door, and slowly pushed it open—just enough so that it could scan the power room's interior.

Two technicians were moving about, both over to its left, approximately fifteen meters away. Fortunately, their line of sight was mostly obscured by large vertical ducts, so they did not see the avatron as it stepped out of the service hatch. It moved quietly across the power room and over to a remote-access terminal that was hidden from view. It jacked-in and went hunting.

Datagrams and schematics flashed across the terminal screen as the avatron went searching for its target. Luca was here somewhere, that much it knew, but now it needed to know her exact location. It hacked into the primary database and found her room—a long-term, ICU. It accessed the camera feed.

A single bed occupied the room, supporting a frail figure covered with a thin sheet. It was Luca Lee-McNabb. The avatron had finally found her. Now it just needed to get to her without being spotted.

It disengaged from the camera in Luca's room and began scanning through other ICU feeds to ascertain what staff were monitoring the patients in the ICU at this time of night.

There was just one: a lone technician sitting in the anti-room of the ICU, monitoring Luca and a number of other patients. But it was already very late and the technician had slumped over the desk, head resting in folded arms, grabbing a quick nap. This was fortuitous, and the avatron wasted no time in hijacking the camera feed for Luca's room and freezing it. The monitor in the observation room went dark for a nanosecond as the live feed was swapped out for a static image.

But before it could continue on its mission, it had one more task to perform. It connected to the New World One comms network and sent three identical messages to three separate recipients. It jacked-out of the terminal and began to seek out a path toward the ICU ward.

LIKE ALL HOSPITALS EVERYWHERE, the nighttime was the quiet time. Even so, a reasonable number of people still worked the nightshift: doctors, nurses, clinicians, porters, technicians, maintenance crews, cleaners, droids, and a host of others whose labors kept the facility running smoothly. And although the avatron had charted a course that avoided the more populated thoroughfares and security cameras, it still needed to be careful not to be spotted at this critical point in its mission. To this end, it had raided a storage room and found a set of overalls used by cleaning staff, along with a peaked cap emblazoned with the New World One hospital insignia. While this disguise did not cover its face, hands, or feet, it might allow it to pass a cursory glance—just another robotic worker going about its business.

The intensive care wing, however, was devoid of people, other than patients—and the lone technician in the observation room. But he was probably still asleep, not that it mattered, since the camera feed from Luca's room had been frozen.

The avatron quietly open the door and entered.

The room was sparse and clinical. A single bed took up most of the central space, surrounded by an array of monitors and medical equipment. The avatron moved over to the side of the bed and looked down at the sleeping figure of Luca Lee-McNabb. Her face was pale, her eyes closed, and her breathing was shallow. An oxygen tube ran up into her nostrils.

It leaned over and, with one hand, gently turned her head so it could examine the base of her skull. With the other hand, it brushed away her hair to reveal a portion of the neural lace that the QI, Athena, had originally given her. The avatron leaned in a little closer and scanned the lace.

The multitude of thin filaments spidering across her skull seemed to have fused themselves with her scalp, and were no doubt the reason why the clinicians treating her had decided to leave it in place.

It reached under the thin sheet, lifted out Luca's left hand, and brought the tip of her index finger up to the control pad on the neural lace. It activated.

The avatron returned her arm to its original resting position, stood upright, and began to scan the RF spectrum, seeking out the interface frequency. Once found, it jacked-in to Luca's mind.

4

CANYONS OF THE MIND

L uca floated face-up in a cool, languid rock pool. The water was clear and fresh, fed by a slow-moving stream running through the canyon. Overhead, a bright sun warmed her face, a light breeze whispered in her ear. Small birds chirped in the trees and bushes lining the banks of the stream. Farther up the slopes she could hear the tinkle of goat bells as they hopped from edge to edge. High up in the clear blue sky, a hawk circled in graceful, effortless arcs. And in that moment, she had never felt more content.

But a new presence entered the canyon. She could sense it in the changing tone of the birdsong, a slight agitation, the chirping of an alert. It seemed to be coming from her left. She pulled her feet up under her and stretched her legs to stand on the sandy bottom of the rock pool, her head and shoulders just above the waterline. She scanned the bank for signs of this new creature that she knew had come. The bushes rustled, and a young boy—or was it a girl, or maybe neither, she wasn't sure—emerged into a clearing on the bank. It stood, smiled at her, and waved. Silence filled the canyon now as the creatures who called it home paused to consider this interloper.

Luca raised a hand and waved back. "Who are you?"

The boy/girl sat down on the sandy bank cross-legged. "I am a messenger from the QI Aria. I've come to take you home."

There was something familiar in the name Aria, but she could not quite remember what it was. "Home?" she asked, a little confused. "But this is my home."

"Then do you remember how you got here?"

Luca laughed a little at this ridiculous question. Even the birds seemed to be laughing as their twittering started up again. Perhaps they assumed this silly creature was no threat, and continued as they were before.

"What a daft question. Of course I do. I..." Luca paused for a moment. "Well...eh..." She couldn't quite put her finger on it. It was there somewhere in her mind, it had to be. But now that this creature had asked her straight out, she found it troubling that she could not answer this simple question. Perhaps it was playing a trick on her, casting some spell.

"What concern is it of yours?" Her voice was harsh and dismissive.

"How long have you been here, in this pool?" The creature gestured at the water.

"I've been here...eh..." Again, Luca found that she did not know. She had no recollection of finding this pool, or wading in for a swim, but she must have—why could she not remember?

The birds seemed to reflect her concern as their chirping became more agitated. They no longer liked this creature; it was bringing disharmony to the canyon.

"Go away, whoever you are. We do not want you here." Luca backed away.

"Have no fear, I am here to help you. I am a friend of the QI Athena. You remember Athena, do you not?"

This name did indeed trigger a memory in Luca's mind. *Athena?* she thought. *How do I know that name?*

"Do you want to see your family again? Miranda and Scott? And your friend, Dr. Rayman?" The creature stood up now and stepped forward, almost to the water's edge.

At the sound of these names, Luca felt a tremor in the canyon. The pool rippled, the sun overhead grew harsher, even the birdsong lost its sweetness. She glanced around, a little concerned.

"What are you doing?" she shouted over to the creature. "You're changing my world. Go away."

"I am not changing it. You are, Luca. This is your dream—you created it." The creature made an expansive gesture with its arms. "It is the safe place you constructed in your mind to shield you from the effects of trauma. You are, in reality, lying in a bed in an intensive care unit in a hospital on the habitat known as New World One."

Luca felt the tremors intensify as the creature

continued, this time pointing at the sky. "The sun above you is the bright ceiling light above your hospital bed. The birdsong and the goat bells are the sounds of the machines monitoring your vitals. The wind whispering down the canyon is the air conditioning unit. The walls of the canyon are the walls of your room."

Luca's world began to transmute as the creature broke down her illusion. The walls of the canyon began to lose their substance, becoming more ethereal. Light and sound began to change, morphing into reality.

But Luca fought back, moving farther out into the pool. She lifted her feet and floated on her back again, looking up at the sky. The sun slowly resumed its warm, steady glow, the birds their cheery chirping, the pool its languid stillness.

"I don't want to leave," Luca said, in a low, almost fragile voice. "I like it here. It's safe."

The creature took a few steps into the water. "I am sorry, Luca, but it is not safe here anymore—and the longer you remain, the more danger you will be in."

Luca turned her head to look at the creature, then rolled over and swam to the edge of the pool. She stood up and gave it a cold, hard look. "It will never end, will it? There will be no future for me save for running and hiding and fighting." Her face grew more troubled and she looked away. "All those dying minds, all that...white noise. All for what?" She snapped around, moved closer, and stared into the dark eyes of the creature. "It will never end. Only when I'm dead, and even then I fear they will find a way to bring me back like some Frankenstein monster."

"I cannot say with any certainty what the future holds, other than you cannot face it by hiding away inside an illusion." The creature met her eyes. "If there is a way to end it, as you say, then you will not find it in here. You must come back. Only then do you have a chance."

Luca cast her gaze around the canyon, savoring the sights, the sounds, the smells. It was just an illusion—in her heart she knew that. She had always known that. She had only intended to tarry here a while, just long enough to replenish her mental strength. Perhaps that time had come, perhaps the creature was right—it was time to go home.

She stepped a little closer to the creature and offered it her hand.

"Very well, I will return."

5

LATE-NIGHT CALLER

A door alert pinged somewhere deep inside Scott McNabb's sleep-addled brain—was it a dream, or was it someone trying to get his attention? His brain shifted up a gear and began turning the wheels for consciousness, starting with audio input analysis. And there it was again—that same alert.

He lifted his head slightly from the pillow and strained to listen. For a moment, there was only silence, accompanied by the sound of his own breathing.

Rat-tat-tat.

Scott sat up on the bed and jerked his head toward the wide windows facing onto the patio at the rear of his accommodation module on New World One. Whoever was trying to get his attention had given up on the front door and now moved on to the back of the building, knocking loudly on the windows. As his eyes began to adjust to the dim light, he could see a human-shaped shadow move through the opaque glass.

Rat-tat-tat.

Scott slowly reached down between the mattress and the headboard of his bed and extracted a plasma pistol. He checked the charge and dialed it up a notch or two above stun. He wasn't taking any chances.

Things had been pretty crazy here ever since the destruction of the QI on Ceres and the attack on New World One. Thousands of new people had migrated to the habitat from Rongo City, all driven by fear of another attack. And even more were arriving from the outlying population centers spread out across this region of the asteroid belt. The situation out there was becoming chaotic and dangerous as various corporations and privateers tried to capitalize on the opportunity presented to them by the loss of the QI.

What passed for government in this neck of the solar system found itself completely out of its depth, struggling to contain the rapidly unfolding situation, having grown soft and impotent after relying on the quantum intelligence on Ceres for over two decades.

So now there was nothing to stop these various interests fighting it out for control over valuable mining resources. As a result, mini-conflicts had broken out all over the region and people were rightly concerned for their safety and that of their families. So a mass exodus was underway. What started as a trickle had now turned into a flood, and New World One was their ark. But it was ill-prepared for this rapid influx. Yes, it was designed to accommodate millions, but the infrastructure was not yet in place to feed and manage all these people. Food was now being rationed until production had a chance to ramp up. But even so, some people were hungry, and prices on the fledgling black market were skyrocketing. As a result, many were desperate and not averse to committing simple acts of burglary as a way to feed their families.

SCOTT RECKONED that whoever was outside right now might simply be trying to ascertain if his place was empty or not. He hefted the pistol, stood up, and made his way to the window. He kept the lights off and his body tight to the wall. The shadow was still out there, moving around, perhaps looking for a way in.

Scott considered just switching on the lights and simply scaring this person away, but another part of him wanted to catch them in the act, or maybe it was just the thrill of the hunt.

Rat-tat-tat.

The shadow had moved closer to the opaque window and was rapping on it again. The figure's outline had become much more defined, and...there was something very familiar about it. He moved a little closer and heard a loud whisper.

"Scott...you lazy bastard, wake up."

Cyrus? he thought. Then quickly slid the door open to find a very irate Cyrus Sanato standing in the pale light, hands on his hips.

"Scott, mind telling me what the hell is going on?"

Scott glanced around, half expecting to see someone else. "What are you doing here?"

Cyrus gave an exasperated gesture with both hands. "What do you mean, what am I doing here? You called me, said it was urgent."

Scott stood dumfounded for a beat. "No I didn't."

They exchanged a split-second look, one that only two friends who know each other's minds can do. A look that said, *Uh-oh. Are you thinking what I'm thinking?*

Scott grabbed his old friend by the arm and pulled him into the building. "Better get inside." He scanned the outside area for a moment. He was in a sparsely built sector of the gargantuan cylindrical habitat, down near the end cap. Some familiar lights flickered here and there in the gloom—nothing out of the ordinary. Scott stepped back inside and slid the door closed.

"I've been trying to contact you for the last hour," Cyrus said with a concerned look on his face. "But there was no connection. I thought that was a bit strange. It's not like you to go dark."

Scott put the plasma pistol down on a countertop and waved a hand over a flat panel to activate a holo-screen. It floated just above the countertop and displayed a list of recent messages. "Connection looks okay. Nothing in from you. Very weird."

Cyrus took a long look at the data displayed on the holo-screen. "I think someone might be playing us. Someone who knows a thing or two about data hacking."

"Maybe it's you they're after, Cyrus. I mean, maybe they wanted you out of that mansion you live in. You know, to rob it."

Cyrus gave a snort. "Best of luck to them if they think they can break in there. It's got a fully armed defense system and a couple of security droids. They're not getting past those without an army."

Scott scratched his chin. "True. Which leaves us with a mystery to solve."

They stood for a moment in the dim light of Scott's living quarters, both contemplating the hidden machinations of this late-night drama when the door alert pinged again.

"Jeez, what now?" Cyrus jerked his head toward the front of the building.

Scott poked the virtual screen and brought up the door camera. "What the..." He grabbed Cyrus's arm and nodded at the image on screen. "It's Miranda and Steph."

Cyrus stood mute for a moment, looking at the screen while his brain tried to compute the meaning of this sudden turn of events.

Scott picked up the plasma pistol and shoved it into Cyrus's hand. "Here, take this, keep it handy. You might need it before the night's out. And go let them in. I need to put on some clothes."

A FEW MOMENTS LATER, Scott returned to the living room, still dimly lit, to find Cyrus, Miranda, and Steph discussing the situation in hushed, concerned tones. They all turned to him as he entered.

"We all got the same identical message...at the exact same time," said Cyrus.

"Someone's trying to get us all together in the one place. Not a good sign." Miranda was busy checking her plasma pistol—something she never went anywhere without these days. Scott suspected she had another, smaller one hidden down the inside of her boot.

"And get us all out by the end cap, out in the sticks. Not many people around here," offered Steph.

"Yeah, in an accommodation module that's half-built with more holes in it than the hull of a smuggler's ship." Miranda was already eyeing up the windows and doors.

Scott pulled another plasma pistol out of a cargo pocket in his newly acquired trousers and handed it to Steph. He had taken it from a stash in a locker under his bed. "Here, take this. I have another." He pulled a second one from another pocket.

She screwed her mouth up and took the pistol, a little hesitantly. "I'd say it's time we all got the hell out of here," she said. "Then we can figure out who's behind all this."

"That would be me."

In an instant, all four plasma pistols were flipped around to point at a tall, robotic avatron sliding back the rear door.

It halted, then gently raised a metallic hand. "Please do not shoot me. That would be most inconvenient."

6

EXODUS

"**Y**ou've got five seconds to explain yourself."
Miranda adopted an assertive stance while
raising the pistol to aim directly at the avatron's
breast plate.

It lowered its hand and stood stock still for a second.
Its cold eyes, if you could call them that, seemed to be
appraising them.

"It's scanning us," said Cyrus.

"Four..." Miranda continued her countdown.

"My apologies for the subterfuge, but secrecy is of the
essence. I could not risk my presence being exposed."
The avatron's voice was low and sonorous.

"Three..." replied Miranda.

"I am a messenger of the quantum intelligence Aria,
of Mars. And I have come to warn you of the approaching
threat to your collective existence."

"Aria?" said Scott, taking a cautious step forward.

"That's impossible. Mars is simply too far away to control an avatron—even for a QI."

"Indeed it is. But I am not controlling this machine directly. I have spent several hours since I established the initial interface reprogramming it to act autonomously as my emissary. So I would appreciate if you would not do anything rash and destroy this avatron, as it will take a considerable amount of time to commandeer another."

"Two..." Miranda reminded everyone.

"Unfortunately, this machine has limited computational power, but I have done my best with what is available, and as such my responses will be limited."

"If you're really Aria, or some fragment of it, then you would have anticipated our skepticism of your story. So how can you prove you are who you say you are?" Scott lowered his weapon a little.

"There are things only you and I know, Scott. Personal conversations that would not be known by some foreign entity pretending to be Aria."

"One..." Miranda stiffened her stance.

Scott glanced over at her and raised a hand. "Let's hear it out."

Miranda threw a glance at Scott, then back to the avatron. Finally, she relaxed a little.

"Do you remember, Scott, on board the Hermes, when you were convinced you were growing a third nipple and you kept asking me for my analysis?"

"Ha ha, that's a good one." Cyrus laughed.

"Seriously?" Miranda gave Scott an incredulous look.

Scott screwed his mouth up and glanced at the floor. "You didn't have to tell them that."

Now Miranda let out a laugh. "That's hilarious." Then she recovered her composure, pointing the weapon at the avatron again.

"Is that true, Scott?" Steph asked.

"Yeah...sort of."

"What do you mean...sort of?" said Miranda.

Scott was silent for a second or two. "Well, I was going through a rough period."

With this admission, a wave of barely concealed sniggering rippled through the ex-crew of the Hermes. Scott jerked his head around to look at them. "That doesn't go outside this room."

"I wouldn't bank on that," replied Miranda, still sniggering. Her attention on the avatron had wavered considerably by now.

"My apologies for embarrassing you in such a manner, Scott," the avatron said with a sympathetic tone, "but as you said, I needed to prove that I am who I claim to be."

Scott fixed a stare at the machine for a second before lowering his weapon. "Okay, you do present a reasonably convincing story, even if it's not one that I wanted out in the open." He turned back to the others. "Everybody else okay with letting this thing continue talking?"

There were muted nods in response.

"Keep your weapon trained on it, Miranda—just in

case," said Scott as he shifted his attention back to the avatron.

"Don't worry, I was planning on doing that anyway." She kept her eyes fixed on the machine.

They moved back into Scott's living quarters, allowing the avatron to fully enter the room. It slid the door closed behind it and sat down on a low sofa, facing the crew. Scott upped the lighting so that he could get a good look at this machine. Miranda held her weapon at the ready.

He recognized it as one of the many used by the New World One executive. State of the art, around two meters tall with a pearlescent sheen on its outer shell. Elegant with strong, exposed titanium joints. Its face, like most avatrons, was minimal, just the barest features with no moving parts, except for the eyes. Its mouth, if you could call it that, was just an impression. Yet it was still an avatron, and as such required direct control.

"How are you doing this?" Scott gestured at the machine. "These things need a user to be connected via a neural link."

"As I said, I reprogrammed it over several hours, and it is limited. However, it is sufficient to serve my purposes."

"Then you'd better get on with it," said Steph, making no effort to disguise her impatience.

"Very well. I took this form so our conversation would remain off-grid. If I were to contact you directly, then apart from the interminably long time-lag, our discussion would be recorded for all to see and hear. But remember,

I am just a fragment of Aria, a mere mote of its consciousness, so I may not be able to answer all your questions." It paused, as if collecting its thoughts before continuing.

"The loss of my compatriot on Ceres has created a power vacuum in this region of the solar system. As we speak, numerous factions are vying for control over lucrative industrial facilities in the asteroid belt, and these skirmishes are growing more violent and intense. Already, New World One is experiencing a second wave of migration, refugees from what is now becoming a war zone. Yet all attempts to reinstate another QI here on the New World are met with political obstruction. Vested interests within the executive see only opportunity in the chaos. They do not want a return to the old order and block all attempts to expedite the installation of a new quantum intelligence."

"We know all this, Aria." Scott shifted forward in his seat. "You didn't go to all this trouble to hack an avatron just to give us a news update."

"Approximately thirty-four hours ago, an interplanetary ship bound for New World One and transporting a new QI from Mars was intercepted in deep space by a well-armed group of mercenaries. They forced their way on board, stole the QI, and disabled the transport so that they could not be followed."

"Stolen! How could you let that happen?" said Scott. "Any idea who they were?"

"Our analysis indicates that they are a group of

privateers known to operate around the Vesta quadrant of the asteroid belt."

"I think I know them," said Miranda. "Guns for hire. A nasty bunch, but very capable."

"So were they working for the VanHeilding Corporation?" asked Cyrus.

"No, at least not directly. We estimate with an eighty-seven percent probability that this was orchestrated by Xiang Zu."

"That's the mining corp?" said Cyrus.

"Correct," replied the avatron with a slight nod of its head.

"What are they playing at? Is it simply ransom?" Miranda lowered her weapon, seeming to now trust the avatron.

"They seek to become the dominant power in the asteroid belt. This, we think, is their ultimate objective. Remember that the VanHeilding Corporation is now beholden to the other members of the seven ruling families, having persuaded them to back their attack on New World One. But the failure to secure a complete takeover left their organization in a weak position. The two ships that led the attack had to limp back to Neo City, the only highly industrialized sector in the solar system that is not controlled by a QI—the only place that was safe for VanHeilding at the time. Yet this necessitated the corporation humbling themselves at the feet of Xiang Zu Corporation who own and control the asteroid city. It is the ultimate humiliation for Fredrick

VanHeilding. As a result, his power and control over the family has been greatly diminished, creating a potential power vacuum. We suspect there will be attempts by others within the family to usurp him and gain power. In essence, the vultures are moving in, picking over the carcass."

"Too bad. And so what? He got what he deserved," said Miranda. "I don't think anyone is going to shed a tear for him."

"What are they planning to do with the QI?" said Scott. "They can't activate it, can they?"

"There are a great many imponderables at this time, but what is clear is that New World One, and the Greater Belt Territories, will fall under the control of the combined forces of the Xiang Zu and VanHeilding Corporations."

"What? That's not going to happen." Cyrus leaped to his feet, becoming more animated at this prospect. "Even without a QI, we've greatly beefed up our defenses. There's no way they could attack us and survive."

The avatron remained composed, pausing for a moment before it began to explain to the former crew of the Hermes the true nature of the threat. "In approximately three months' time, the asteroid enclave of Neo City will reach the apogee of its solar orbit, which will bring it very close to this sector of the asteroid belt. This is when we calculate they will launch an attempted takeover of New World One. This leaves insufficient time for us to fabricate a new QI and have it shipped here. So to repel an attack, you will be exclusively relying on superior firepower."

"Exactly. And we have that—in spades." Cyrus was emphatic.

"Yes, but will you use it?"

"What do you mean by that?" Scott became curious of the avatron's line of thinking.

"The subjugation of the less powerful families who control resource extraction in the asteroid belt is now underway by Xiang Zu. Without raw materials, the New World project is dead. So who in the executive will stop them if they choose to take over?"

There was silence in the room as this prospect began to sink in. It was becoming clear to Scott that by stealing the QI, the final chess move had been made. Everything that now happened was just one more move toward checkmate. The avatron was right: the end was inevitable.

"So what do we do?" Scott asked in the tone of one who knows when they're facing hard choices.

"I was once the artificial intelligence that controlled the science vessel Hermes. In that capacity, my primary directive was for the welfare of my crew. Even though that ship is long gone and my obligations now extend to the entirety of the planet Mars and its environs, my primary directive still stands. I have taken this extraordinary step of utilizing an avatron to bring you this warning: If you remain on New World One, you will be trapped by agents of VanHeilding or Xiang Zu, and you will be killed. You need to take the ship Perception and get out now—chart a course to Mars, where you will be safe under my protection."

"It seems that human civilization is regressing back to the bad old days." Steph gave a long sigh.

"Is there nothing the QI network can do?" Miranda asked.

"Our power is waning. Attacks on our infrastructure are escalating as new node-runners are being developed. One of our number has been destroyed, and even Solomon on Europa grows ever more distant. There is little we can to do prevent the takeover of New World One."

"Then we have no choice," said Scott. "We must leave as soon as possible."

"Yes, but be warned, it will not be without danger. Once your ship leaves the protection of the habitat, it will be stalked by those who seek to claim the price that is on all your heads. And there may be lesser members of the VanHeilding family who might view your capture as a way to move up the ranks. You must be vigilant."

"What about Luca?" said Miranda. "She still hasn't awoken from her catatonic state, and deep-space travel could just make the condition worse."

The avatron again paused for a moment before announcing, "You will find that that is no longer a problem."

"What do you mean?" Miranda became agitated. "What have you done?"

"If you check with the hospital, you will find that Luca is now awake and fully conscious."

Miranda jumped up from her seat. "Awake? But... how... How is that possible?"

"Does it matter?" replied the avatron.

Scott exchanged glances with Miranda, while Steph was already fishing out her comms unit to verify the avatron's assertion that Luca had indeed regained consciousness. A brief moment later, a look of incredulity crossed her face. She looked over at Scott and Miranda.

"It's true. She has returned."

7

ZEROBALL

eroBall is a sport played by either the reckless or the desperate, or both. Exclusive to the artificial-gravity environment of Neo City, it has become extremely popular by virtue of its propensity to severely injure its participants—sometimes fatally. Yet this does not deter the high numbers of citizens partaking in the sport, primarily because the prize money is so eye-watering—more than enough to entice the reckless and the desperate to risk a broken neck.

Like most spectator sports, it is a team effort that involves trying to get a ball across the opponent's line. In the case of ZeroBall, that line is simply a round hoop into which the ball must be placed in order to score. In a way, it is similar to basketball, but that's where the similarity ends, since this is not played on the ground but in midair, in zero-gee.

Neo City is a unique habitat within the solar system

in that it is carved out of an asteroid. It has an internal diameter of over a half-kilometer, and because it spins around the central axis, this creates an artificial gravity on the inner rim similar to Earth.

However, with the help of a gas-powered thruster pack and enough elevation, a person could lift themselves off the ground, so to speak, then apply a directional force opposite to that of the spin, and they would be weightless. From there they could soar up and around the interior volume on nothing more than a puff of expelled gas.

In practice, though, people who want to experience these weightless acrobatics generally travel up to the central axis using one of the end cap elevators. This would drain their stored angular velocity and render them weightless. Then, all that is needed is for them to launch themselves into empty space and fly around using any form of low-powered thruster.

Yet they have to be careful not to fly too close to the ground, since they could be sideswiped by a structure such as the side of a building as it rotates with the spin of the habitat. This is because, with an outer rotational speed of one-point-three RPM, that structure will hit them at over two hundred kilometers per hour—an impact of such force that few live to tell the tale.

Yet despite all the inherent dangers, this was a pastime that many people in Neo City engaged in simply for the pleasure—being careful to stick to the center of the habitat and not get too close to the edges. And, like all human pastimes, it wasn't long before it generated a slew of competitive sports. The most popular of these being ZeroBall.

Each team consists of five players, and the objective is to place a ball through a hoop at the end of the opposing team's half. The hoops are one-meter-diameter light projections, and the field length is a half-kilometer. The actual ball is made of a hard, polished metallic alloy, large enough that it cannot be gripped with just one hand. As a consequence of this design, players tend to hold it to their chest or tuck it under one arm.

The ball also has an autonomously controlled safety feature that prevents it from spiraling out of control and smashing into the inner rim of the habitat. This autonomy also allows for a random change of direction every now and again, just to mix things up. If, during a game, the ball is simply floating in free space, it may suddenly fly off in a new direction, sending the players scrambling to alter their flight vector to chase it down— usually to the whoops and cheers of the spectators.

To add a little more danger to the sport, as if it wasn't dangerous enough, a series of one-hundred-meter-tall poles telescope up from the floor of the habitat, spaced one hundred meters apart. These are semi-flexible and padded, so that being side-swiped by the top of one of these would not result in anything more damaging than some bruising. However, any player who has the misfortune to hit one would almost certainly be sent into an uncontrolled tumble. This is the greatest fear of any player—to be spinning around with no idea of up or down or direction of travel. A tumble can also occur when two players impact in a tussle to get hold of the ball. In fact, it is a strategy adopted by all players to destabilize and disorient their opponent.

But there was one important rule that had to be introduced early on in the game's development, and that was the *quid pro quo* rule. This meant that if a player was incapacitated for some reason, and needed to retire from the field, then a player from the opposing team also had to retire. This rule was introduced to prevent teams trying to eliminate each other by simply sending their opponents crashing to the ground or forcing them to hit one of the poles. Such a game would have an unacceptably high fatality count, with the winner literally being the last person standing—or floating, in this case. Yet it was still a dangerous game, and fatal injuries were not uncommon.

TODAY WAS ZERODAY—THE day of the final match of the tournament, when the two top teams would fight it out for the grand prize. A cash amount that would allow every player on the winning team to never have to worry about money again. Everything in Neo City came to a standstill on ZeroDay. Everybody who could stopped work, and a carnival atmosphere took over the entire habitat— with buildings and streets festooned with team colors as the build-up to the final reached fever pitch.

All citizens were expected to join in the festivities, and that even included Fredrick VanHeilding, much to his annoyance. It wasn't that he disliked the game or the carnival atmosphere—it was because he would have to show his face at a party organized by the governor of Neo City, Lui Wei, a high-ranking member of the ruling Xiang Zu family.

After beating a hasty retreat from the failed attempt at taking control of New World One, VanHeilding limped away and sought sanctuary at Neo City. This made him beholden to Lui Wei and the Xiang Zu family—and Fredrick did not like being beholden to anyone. By attending the party, he would be allowing Lui Wei an opportunity to belittle him, by making him acutely aware of his family's reliance on the support and generosity of Xiang Zu Corporation.

A sleek, private gyro gracefully touched down inside the VanHeilding compound in Neo City—a sizable chunk of real estate that the family had managed to carve out for themselves over many decades of involvement in the asteroid city-state. The gyro was a small, airborne craft of simple design, a cabin suspended beneath four sets of counter-rotating blades, one at each corner. Dispatched courtesy of Lui Wei, it arrived to pick up Fredrick and his entourage and bring them to the game. This would be one of the last flights of the day, before all aerial activity was suspended for the duration of the event.

The side door of the gyro swung up to reveal a

luxurious interior. Two Xiang Zu operatives, dressed in the understated elegance of the very rich, hopped out. One scanned the area while the other escorted Fredrick into the private cabin along with Sebastian VanHeilding, a distant cousin of Fredrick's—a midranking member of the family. The third member of Fredrick's entourage, a trusted bodyguard and node-runner who went by the name of César, also took up a seat in the gyro. The door closed with a hiss and the sleek machine powered up its quad rotors.

As the craft rose into the Neo City sky, beginning its short journey to Lui Wei's residence, Fredrick gazed out the window at the crowds gathered in the streets down below. Everywhere he looked was thronged with ordinary people in full party mode: drinking, singing, dancing, and generally having a good time.

"Looks like one heck of a party going on down there," said Sebastian, also gazing down at the revelers through a window on the opposite side of the cabin.

"Yes, their one day of joy in an otherwise mundane and turgid existence." He said this as if speaking to himself.

"You almost sound like you feel sorry for them." Sebastian turned his head away from the window.

Fredrick frowned. "Perhaps I do. Perhaps I feel sorry for their ignorance, their pursuit of the baser pleasures. That which gratifies the body rather than the mind."

This response seemed to silence Sebastian, since he

did not reply and instead returned to gazing out the window at the crowd below.

The gyro slowed and came to a hover over the landing pad in the sprawling Lui Wei compound. It rotated gently and descended to a soft touchdown on one of the upper decks. The compound occupied a central position within Neo City and was built over several different levels, perfect as a ringside seat for the ZeroBall final.

Fredrick and Sebastian exited the craft and were ushered down a broad stairway onto a wide lido deck, populated with a generous scattering of the rich and beautiful of Neo City. Some gathered around the bars and tables, others draped themselves decoratively across sofas and recliners. All were abuzz with an excited anticipation of the forthcoming game.

But their path continued through this privileged throng of Neo City citizens and down a few short steps to a roped-off VIP deck—the prime location in all of Neo City to watch the day's events unfold. The VanHeildings were shown to their seats, each an oversized circular sofa. They settled in, and refreshments were brought.

Fredrick cast a glance around at the other VIPs assembled here; most were members of the seven most powerful families in the solar system. He nodded polite greetings to those he knew.

"We have arrived in a nest of vipers," Fredrick whispered over to Sebastian, who was busy adjusting his ample frame into a comfortable position on the sofa.

"Good view, though." He glanced up at the game area

above, then back at the party on the upper deck. "No sign of our esteemed host yet."

Before Fredrick could answer, a blast of triumphant music reverberated around the game area, and with it all eyes turned to look up at them. Fredrick glanced back to see Lui Wei entering along with several others. Some were clearly bodyguards, and others merely fashion accessories. He strolled past the rows of sofas to the edge of the deck and waved to the thongs of people below. A loud cheer could be heard echoing around the habitat. After a moment or two of soaking up the adulation, Lui Wei turned away from the edge and made himself comfortable in the central seat, just an arm's reach away from Fredrick.

"Glad you could make it, Fredrick." He said this without turning his head. He was still waving and smiling at the crowd.

"How could I miss the final of the most renowned tournament in the entire solar system?"

"You flatter us. Our game is but a humble trial of zero-gravity skill."

Before Fredrick could reply, a deafening cheer erupted from the crowd as players began entering the game area high above. They flew in from both ends of the of the giant habitat, five players on each side, waving to the crowd as they flew by. From Fredrick's perspective, and all those who watched from around the rim of the habitat, the players seemed to spin slowly as they progressed toward each other. But in reality they were stationary; it was the habitat that spun around the players. Fredrick found himself a little awed by this phenomenon of physics, despite his overall disinterest in the game.

The players were dressed in slick, skintight bodysuits designed to afford minimal opportunity for an opponent to grab on to them. Small gas thrusters were strapped to each forearm, allowing them to maneuver in free space. But gas reserves were restricted, requiring the player to be efficient and frugal in their use. One team wore all yellow, the other all green. They slowed to a floating stop, taking up positions prior to commencement of the game. A palpable wave of excitement rippled throughout the crowd, and all eyes again turned to Lui Wei. He stood up, walked to the edge, and raised a hand in the air. The crowd settled down to a murmur. High overhead, a shiny metallic sphere zoomed to a point in space equidistant from the two teams, then stopped and hovered there, motionless.

Lui Wei took a moment to survey the crowd, allowing the thrill of anticipation to build, his arm raised high above his head. "Let the game...begin." He shouted the last word, bringing his hand down in one swift movement at the same time. The crowd roared their approval as a player from each team broke off and made a beeline for the sphere. Wei sat down again and settled in.

Despite his natural cynicism, Fredrick VanHeilding found himself enthralled by the game as it progressed. It was physics as ballet, Newtonian mechanics as entertainment. He barely noticed the twenty minutes of play pass by before the first-quarter horn blew. Both teams had so far failed to score.

The noise from the crowd began to settle down as they took the opportunity to discuss the game so far and stock up on vitals prior to recommencement of battle. Lui Wei leaned over toward Fredrick. "Enjoying our humble sport?"

"I must admit, I find it quite captivating."

"Ahh...but they're only getting warmed up. Wait until the last quarter when they become more desperate." He cocked an eye over at Sebastian. "And what brings you to our asteroid city?"

"I've heard so much about this famous game of ZeroBall, and I was in the neighborhood, so to speak. So I decided on a whim to come and see it for myself." Sebastian's demeanor was jovial. He was clearly enjoying the game.

"In the neighborhood? How fortunate." Lui Wei glanced at Fredrick with a skeptical look, then back at Sebastian. "That's a very fine ship you have," he continued. "I don't think I've ever seen one quite like it."

Sebastian shifted in his seat, clearly proud that Lui Wei had noticed the splendor of his vessel. "It's the very latest from the Cerellian Engineering Shipyards, designed to my own specification, and the fastest in the system."

"Then you must meet our chief ship designer. I imagine you two would have much to talk about. He'll be at the grand gala at the end of the tournament. You are coming, aren't you?"

"Eh...I'm afraid not. We'll be leaving tomorrow."

"Ah...that's unfortunate." Wei remained silent for a moment, preferring to adjust the placement of his drink on the small table beside him.

He turned to Fredrick and leaned in close. "I heard a rumor," he finally said, his voice low and serious. "A rumor that your wayward daughter and her entourage have left the relative safety of New World One, bound for Mars, I believe." He turned and gave Fredrick a considered look. "Interesting development, don't you think? A person might get tempted, thinking of them out there...all alone and isolated."

So there it is, thought Fredrick. *This is what's bothering him.* "I've heard that rumor too, and maybe that's what they want a person to believe...that they're all alone, ready to be picked off."

"Ahh...you are the wily one, Fredrick. Always thinking of plots within plots."

They stopped talking, since the second quarter was about to begin. It opened with a bang. Yellow were quicker off the mark and snagged the sphere first. A few deft passes later and the first score of the game was chalked up—the yellow fans roared their approval. Green was now under pressure, and so came out swinging. They were first to the sphere this time, and getting more aggressive. A deft turn and a well-timed kick by a green player sent one of the opposing team tumbling uncontrollably into the path of a rotating pole. The crowd held their breath, then let out a collective sigh as the player managed to correct course, missing the oncoming pole by a whisker.

Again, Fredrick became enthralled by this gear shift in the game, so much so that he almost put all thoughts of Wei's inquisition out of his mind.

But as the second-quarter horn sounded, Wei continued, "As you know, Neo City will be at its closest point to New World One in less than three months." He gave Fredrick another of his considered looks. "It wouldn't be good to get distracted from our ultimate mission."

By now, Fredrick was getting a little annoyed at the subtext of this conversation. Was Lui Wei really so emboldened as to presume to question VanHeilding family business? True, the Xiang Zu clan had invested heavily in the success of the first mission, and had also facilitated the rebuild of the two VanHeilding ships. But this did not give him the authority, in Fredrick's mind, to dictate what he should or should not do.

"Agreed," Fredrick finally replied with clenched teeth.

But Lui Wei persisted. "If the Perception has indeed departed for Mars, then surely that is one less thing to concern ourselves with?"

Fredrick carefully considered his response. On the one hand, he did not want to open up a fissure between the two families. But on the other, he did not like being lectured by this arrogant fop.

"These are family matters." He gave a nonchalant, dismissive gesture. "No need for you to concern yourself with them."

"But of course. Please forgive my intrusion." Wei gave an apologetic smile. "I'm merely saying that it is never good to get sidestepped into adventures whose objectives many would consider a distraction."

Fredrick remain silent, and seriously considered getting up and leaving the game. But that was probably not a good idea. So he simply ignored Lui Wei's taunts. Fortunately, the third quarter of the game was about to begin.

IT OPENED with the score still even at five points each. But the lure of the prize money must have been on the players' minds during recess, since both teams found yet another gear. Straight out of the gate, the play was faster and even more aggressive this time around.

Within the first minute of play commencing, a green player had been forced into the path of an oncoming pole and looked to be knocked unconscious with the impact. She bounced off in an uncontrolled tumble, heading toward the inner rim. The crowd rose to their feet in anticipation of a fatal smash, but the player managed to come to, regain control, and made her way back to the play area. There was a hint of disappointment from the crowd at being denied this drama.

Yet, the player had clearly been injured and seemed to have difficulty getting oriented. Yellow's blood was now up, and in the intervening moment had managed to score another point, putting them in the lead. But green were not giving up just yet, and a battle royale played out for the remaining quarter. Nevertheless, it ended 6-5 to yellow.

This only added to Fredrick's irritation as both he and Sebastian, at Lui Wei's request, had taken a flutter on the game, picking green to win. Whereas he, of course, had chosen yellow.

"Looks like your team is struggling, Fredrick."

"It's not over yet," he snapped back.

"True, there's still plenty to fight for." He paused for a beat, then leaned in closer to Fredrick and lowered his voice. "Concerning our earlier conversation, it would be remiss of me if I did not inform you that some of the lesser families invested in our...endeavor are getting a little anxious."

Fredrick replied with a quick wave of his hand as if swatting a fly. "But we both know they are fools. I for one see nothing but success in securing New World One. To my mind it is inevitable."

"My own sentiments exactly," said Lui Wei. "And it would seem that your estranged family think likewise by beating a hasty exit before they are trapped." Wei considered his next words for a moment. "But what's concerning the other families is why you failed the first time, considering that the QI on Ceres was destroyed."

Fredrick returned a glare. "I'm not in the mood right now to explain what happened all over again."

"No, of course not. We're here to enjoy ourselves." Wei paused for a beat. "But I've been hearing some...wild stories, rumors of a *ghost in the machine.* Utter nonsense, I imagine, but they do persist."

"It's complete drivel. I can't imagine where you heard that," Fredrick returned.

"Oh, people talk. Especially in bars and clubs. Your node-runners are still only human—they like to socialize just like everyone else. They drink, they let their hair down, they talk."

"Well, it's absurd."

"I'm sure it is. But what's intriguing is that the name Luca has been mentioned, more than once. And spoken of in hushed, reverent tones—so I've been told. This is your granddaughter, I believe. What do you make of that?"

After the failure to capture New World One, Fredrick had kept quiet about the power that Luca wielded. For one, would anyone really believe that a single person could undermine the combined processing power of a well-trained cohort of node-runners? Fredrick gave another dismissive gesture. "Excuses, excuses. They simply overplayed their hand taking out the QI and left themselves with insufficient resources to finish the job. That's not going to happen again."

But Fredrick's final worlds were drowned out by the

roar of the crowd as the players took their positions for the final quarter of the game.

THE FINAL CHAPTER in this aerial battle opened with a frenzied rush for the sphere, with several players from both sides making a dash for possession. Their combined efforts resulted in a ruck of bodies spinning and tumbling as each player fought for control. This seemed to please the crowd to no end, as they cheered and hooted their approval.

One body eventually escaped from the ruck with the sphere and made a beeline for the yellow end. The remaining players tussled with each other, green trying to break free while yellow tried to hold them back. But the player with possession was not having it all his own way. An opponent was hot on his heels and gaining.

The crowd cheered on the chase, applauding and groaning in equal measure as their team won or lost control of the sphere. The game had become a messy affair, with both sides willing to physically block or attack their opponents with a sense of wild abandon. It was the last quarter and caution had been discarded. Every player was now all in.

Sebastian had totally succumbed to the emotional rollercoaster of the game, cheering like the best of them when green had possession, booing when they lost it. Even Fredrick could not help himself when green finally evened the score. He rose from his seat, clapping and cheering without realizing it.

Lui Wei called over to him when he finally sat back down.

"It's all to play for now, the next blow will win the game and take the prize. But does your team have what it takes, Fredrick? Or will they be like your node-runners and fail at the last hurdle?"

The answer came in the last seconds as a green player closed in on the hoop, poised to take the winning point, only to run out of gas for their thrusters. With no way to correct course, they shot too soon and missed.

With one player now out of commission, the yellow team grabbed their chance, and in three swift passes had the sphere back at the opposite end and into the hoop, just as the final horn sounded.

Sebastian threw his hands up in the air in despair, while Fredrick seethed. Wei leaned over to commiserate. "Bad luck, old boy. Seems your team didn't leave enough in the tank to finish the job."

8

SHIPPING OUT

Regardless of Lui Wei's taunting of Fredrick at the ZeroBall final, he had been growing increasingly frustrated just knowing that Luca, along with the entire former crew of the science vessel Hermes, were out there, just waiting to be taken. Yet he was not in a position to do anything about it. All his resources were dedicated to the renewed assault on New World One, and much as he hated to admit it, Lui Wei was right: this was not the time to get distracted. If he were to divert one of his ships now and go after them, it would not go down well with the other families. In reality, he would just be giving them an opportunity to undermine VanHeilding's grip on power.

Already, Xiang Zu Corporations were making hay out in the asteroid belt, taking over outposts, eliminating competitors, and generally causing chaos. Once the full complement of ships arrived in a few months, they would surely have total control of all the Belt's resources. Provided, of course, that VanHeilding took control of the habitat.

Yet it was not all bad news, either. Particularly since his treacherous daughter, Miranda, had decided to abandon New World One and take Luca to Mars. So with Luca out of the way, he was virtually guaranteed success in taking control of the habitat. Yet somewhere in the back of his mind, he couldn't help thinking that it could all be just a ruse by Miranda. A trick to make him believe they had left, only for his new armada to face the power of Luca's extraordinary node-running abilities once again. There was no way that he could risk walking into a trap like that. Xiang Zu were already waiting in the long grass, ready to pounce given any opportunity. If Fredrick failed to take control of New World One again, he would give them that excuse. It would be the beginning of the end for the family.

Nonetheless, some of the stories coming out of New World One were that Luca was in a coma, with little or no sign of recovery. But again, this could simply be a bogus story put out there just to set him up. What Fredrick really needed was clarity. He needed to know precisely where Luca was, and her true mental state. Was she actually on the Perception like he was supposed to believe, or lying in wait on the habitat, or was she somewhere else entirely?

. . . ,

ALL THIS UNCERTAINTY weighed heavily on Fredrick's mind as he made his way on a personal shuttle out to Sebastian VanHeilding's fancy-assed ship, Daedalus, which was still parked in close proximity to Neo City. He would be leaving soon to continue his so-called *grand tour* of the solar system, heading to Mars for the Festival of Lights. This presented Fredrick with an opportunity—that is, if he could trust Sebastian not to screw it up.

The ship, an M3-class luxury interplanetary transport built by Cerellian Engineering Shipyards, was indeed a thing of beauty. Sleek, elegant, almost organic, with a purposeful-looking engine array. Yet it was small and lacked a gravity ring—a rotating torus that provided the occupants with simulated gravity. However, this was not some flaw in its design, but a feature that allowed the ship to land on any body within the solar system with a gravity well less than one-third that of Earth's. This meant it could land on Mars, hence the M3 classification. It was also fast, possibly one of the fastest in the entire solar system—as Sebastian VanHeilding so often crowed about to anyone who would listen.

The shuttle slowed to a halt directly over a docking port on the ship's topside, then rotated slightly to orient itself for correct alignment. Both shuttle and ship were now operating autonomously, making all the micro-adjustments needed to allow the umbilical to telescope up from the docking and make a secure connection. Alerts sounded in the cockpit, and the pilot called back to

Fredrick, "Docking complete, sir. Opening the hatch now."

As Fredrick floated over to the hatch, he considered how much he hated zero-gee; it was unnatural and disorienting. He could not understand how anyone would spend an entire journey in deep space with absolutely no gravity—the concept was beyond him. Yet it seemed that the zero-gee experience was becoming more fashionable these days. With faster engines and shortened transfer times, it was now the favored mode of travel for a new generation seeking out the "real" space-travel experience.

The hatch door swung open, and after some help from the pilot, Fredrick managed to float through into the ship. Sebastian was waiting for him on the other side, smiling like a child at a fairground, no doubt delighted at the opportunity to show off his elegant ship.

"Fredrick, so glad you decided to come for the guided tour." Sebastian extended a welcoming arm.

"I'm not here to get a tour of your goddamn ship."

Sebastian's face morphed into one of near heartbreak.

"I only came here so we could have a discussion in private, away from the snooping of Lui Wei and Xiang Zu."

Sebastian regained some composure and shook his head. "You don't want to see the ship?"

Fredrick replied by way of an angry glare.

"I see," said Sebastian. "Very well, follow me to the bridge. We can talk there."

. . .

As THEY FLOATED through the ship en route to the bridge, Fredrick was surprised by how spacious it was. From the outside it seemed small, but perhaps that was just a trick of design. Yet now that he was moving along its corridors, he sensed it could carry at least fifty or more people in comfort, as well as a reasonable complement of rovers and drones. He found himself becoming more impressed with the craft as he progressed—not that he would let Sebastian know this. It would only inflate his already overblown ego even more.

The bridge also had an odd design, one Fredrick had never seen before. But as he cast his eyes around the space, he could see that since this ship could land on a planet, it needed to be able to accommodate this. So, unlike ships that spent all their time in space, where up/down had no meaning, this had a very definite up-and-down orientation. Yet it also had a multitude of grips and handles to assist moving in zero-gee.

He moved himself onto a seat and strapped in so that he would not have to hold on to something to keep himself oriented. Sebastian, on the other hand, preferred to simply float with one hand holding the edge of the central holo-table.

Fredrick settled himself in and gave his distant cousin a long, cold stare. "So why are you really here, Sebastian? And don't give me that bullshit about wanting to see the famous game of ZeroBall."

GERALD M. KILBY

"What do you mean?" He feigned umbrage. "Isn't ZeroBall a good enough reason?"

"I said don't bullshit me." Fredrick glared at him.

Sebastian remained silent for a moment, looking at something on the holo-table. "The family thought you could do with some...moral support, now that we need to kowtow to Xiang Zu." He looked around to face Fredrick, returning his glare.

Fredrick pursed his lips and sighed. "So you were sent here to spy on me, report back on my state of mind, I suppose?"

"No, nothing as vulgar as that. But they are...how shall I put it...concerned that the foundations of our power are being mortgaged."

"They seek to undermine my authority?"

"There are rumblings of discontent. Factions are forming, some who think the quest to acquire New World One is a game where the stakes are simply too high."

"And you, where do you stand?"

Sebastian gave a broad smile. "Fortune favors the bold."

Fredrick considered this response for a moment. It could have several meanings, not least Sebastian's *bold* desire to rise up the family ranks. But that was common knowledge; Sebastian didn't try to hide his ambition, which was partly why Fredrick put up with him. At least he knew where he stood.

"Fortune may well favor the bold, as you put it, Sebastian. But it can also get you killed." Fredrick leaned

64

in a little and nodded. "You would do well to remember that."

Sebastian glanced down at the holo-table again, gathering his thoughts. "So let me ask you the same question then, Fredrick. Why are you here...on my ship? What is it you want to discuss?"

It was now Fredrick's turn to pause and gather his thoughts as he contemplated his proposal. It was risky. Could he trust Sebastian to pull this off without his ego and ambition getting in the way? But as he ran through all the possible permutations in his mind, Sebastian and his fancy ship could be utilized for a far greater purpose than simply pursuing a decadent lifestyle.

"I'm offering you a chance to do your duty for the family. To do something that will allow you to rise up through the ranks. Perhaps even gain a seat at the high table."

Sebastian smiled, his eyes widened, and he gave an expansive gesture with his free hand. "I'm all ears."

Fredrick unstrapped himself from the seat and floated over to the holo-table. After a moment familiarizing himself with its operation, he brought up a 3D rendering of the local solar system, a standard navigation map. He pointed to a line that scribed itself through open space. "This is the estimated flight path of the Perception, en route to Mars, as you can see here." He pointed at the line. "Do you think this ship can intercept it?"

"So you're going after Luca. I knew it."

"No, I'm not going after her, not yet. I just need to establish if she's actually on this ship. So can you intercept it or not?"

Sebastian entered some data into the navigation chart and a new line appeared, emanating from Neo City. "Yes, it seems we can." He glanced at Fredrick with a broad smile.

"Good, very good." He gave Sebastian a careful look. "Understand that establishing Luca's presence on that ship is critical to our planned takeover of New World One. All indications suggest that she is on it, but that may just be a ruse, something they want us to believe. It may be that, in reality, she's lying in wait for us at New World One, and that would be a challenging situation, to say the least."

Sebastian nodded. "I understand. But even if we intercept the Perception, how will we know if she is on board?"

"I'm giving you one of my top node-runners, César Castello. You need to get your ship close enough so that he can do a probe of the Perception. Remember, this was once a VanHeilding ship before Miranda stole it, so it should be possible."

Sebastian gestured toward a side bay on the bridge, with two node-runner terminals. "I already have two of my own, both at the top of their game. Why do I need another?"

"You have no idea who you're dealing with here, Sebastian. If Luca is really on that ship, and she's even half-functioning, any contact with her by an inexperienced node-runner would just end in potential brain death. Trust me, no matter how highly you think of your people, they are no match for her. Let César initiate the probe. Your people can back him up under his direction."

Sebastian looked at Fredrick with wide eyes. "So the rumors are true, then. She is this *ghost in the machine* that all the node-runners fear?"

Fredrick gave his distant cousin a considered look. "What I'm about to tell you, Sebastian, is above your current rank. But since you are accepting this mission, I feel it's only right that you should know the truth. Do I have your word that you will keep what I'm about to tell you a closely guarded secret?"

"Of course. You have my word."

"Very well. As you probably know, Luca's my granddaughter. One of hundreds that I have, all of whom are the product of a generational experiment in quantum biology. You see, the family have been working for a very long time to create an enhanced node-runner. One who can utilize quantum effects and operate more like a QI. However, all our efforts came to naught, except for Luca. The irony in all of this is that her inception was natural, as opposed to all the others, which were lab-grown."

"So...would I be right in assuming that she was on New World One when we attacked, but nobody realized her abilities...until she entered the habitat's data-stream?"

Fredrick was mildly impressed with Sebastian's analysis. Perhaps there was more to him than met the eye. Maybe this *indolent fop* persona of his was all just an act, in which case Fredrick may do well to keep him close.

"You are correct. But I don't think she knew, either, so we were all caught off-guard—we won't make that mistake again. That said, if the intelligence we've been receiving is correct, she was greatly weakened by the encounter and is believed to be in a coma. But that too could be just a bullshit story. So it's critical that you find out if she's really on that ship, and not setting up an ambush on New World One."

Sebastian nodded. "Understood."

"And listen"—Fredrick jabbed an index finger at him —"if she does prove to be on that ship, don't get any ideas above your rank. Do not, under any circumstances, try and take her on. You will almost certainly fail. Is that clear?"

Sebastian seemed a little hesitant in his response. "But what if it turns out she really is in a coma, as they say she is? Surely it would be an opportunity not to be missed, to capture her while she's exposed and isolated in deep space?"

"I appreciate how tempting that scenario might be, and believe me, capturing her is the ultimate objective. But now is not the time, and you do not have the resources to take on the Perception. Don't forget, Miranda turned it into a den of mercenaries—it's a veritable warship. It's well armed and would cut you to shreds. So stay well away. All I need is for you to establish if Luca is on it. That way, we can proceed with the invasion of New World One with confidence. Once that's achieved, then we can develop a more comprehensive plan to acquire Luca."

Again, Sebastian hesitated before replying. "Very well. We'll depart in a few hours, as soon as the ship is finished with the resupply."

Fredrick nodded and moved away from the holo-table, heading for the exit. He turned to look back at the doorway. "Don't let me down on this mission, Sebastian. And more importantly, don't let the family down. This is your chance to prove that you're more than just the decadent playboy you let people believe you are."

9

AUXILIARY COMMAND

L uca sat cross-legged on a packing crate, one of a great many that now occupied the old swimming pool on the interplanetary ship Perception. She remembered the pool from her early childhood—how it used to be in all its grandeur. But it had fallen into disuse as the ship became home to a crew of mercenaries who had no use for such luxuries. It was now part storeroom, part workshop, part boneyard. The crates and supplies were needed to balance the weight on the torus, according to Cyrus, so the old pool was now just a storage bunker.

Yet Luca still liked this place. It was the largest open space on the ship, and it had a gloriously wide window where she could look out at the universe beyond. She sat and gazed out at the stars, trying to imagine that she could see Mars, although this was impossible since they were still much too far away.

They had left New World One twenty-nine days ago and spent the first three days burning hard, trying to shake any ships that might try and follow them, taking heavy-gee in the process. They kept this up intermittently for a further fifteen days until everyone was utterly exhausted and simply couldn't take any more.

Nevertheless, two ships still tracked them, not far behind. Quite what these ships hoped to achieve was questionable since the Perception had considerable firepower on board, more than enough to deal with scavengers and bounty hunters. Miranda reckoned that they were just opportunists, hoping that something might happen to the ship, a technical failure or meteorite strike. Then they would pounce. Yet no one seemed that concerned about these pursuers.

Of more concern was Neo City. Soon they would be at their closest point in space to the asteroid enclave as it made its orbital journey closer to the Belt region of space. This was where VanHeilding had retreated to, and if the family were going to make a move on them, then it would more likely be coming from Neo City, and soon. So for the last four days, they had all been resting up in anticipation of a further heavy burn, the longest of the journey so far, which should keep them ahead of any opportunists from Neo City who had aspirations of catching them.

Nobody was looking forward to it, least of all Luca, who had still not regained her full strength after her seven-month-long coma. She lay down flat on her back on the packing crate, rested her head on her hands, and contemplated the ceiling. She tried to imagine herself back in the pool in the canyon, cool and languid, timeless and safe.

But her daydream was interrupted by the sound of the doors to the pool room opening, followed by the sound of short, skipping footsteps. She recognized them as belonging to Cyrus.

He did not see her, as she had the more elevated position. She tapped the neural lace at the base of her skull and activated it. She could now see the camera feed from her drone, Fly, which had perched itself high up on one of the ducts that ran along the ceiling of the pool room.

Cyrus was checking labels on a row of packing crates, looking for something, muttering to himself as he went. One of the ship's service droids followed as he moved along the rows. Eventually, he arrived at a point just below Luca.

She lifted herself up on one elbow and looked down at him. "Hi, Cyrus, what you up to?"

He jumped back, startled. "Jeez, Luca. Don't do that. You scared the crap out of me."

"Oops, sorry." She sat up, legs dangling over the edge of the crate.

"Eh...I'm trying to find a spare part. It's supposed to be here somewhere."

"What for? Something break? Hope it's not important."

"Ahh...this entire ship is falling apart." He scanned another label, then looked up again at Luca. "Don't worry, nothing major. It's just I might be able to get us a shade more power by replacing some of the control boards for the starboard containment vessel."

"I see. It wouldn't be good if we had a plasma containment failure during the next heavy burn."

Cyrus moved on to the next packing crate. "That almost never happens these days. Mostly this type of ship drive just loses oomph over time."

"You worried about what could start chasing us down from the Neo City asteroid?"

Cyrus glanced up at Luca and gave her a considered look, although it was hard to tell since he permanently wore an ocular visor. "I'd be lying if I said I wasn't." He spun his head around to look at the droid, who had been scanning along a different row of crates. "Ahh...I think we've found one." He moved over the droid and scanned the label. "Bingo."

Luca clambered down from her perch atop the crates and came over. "Can I help? I'm pretty good with tools. I think people forget I'm a technologist. It's what I did before...well, you know."

"Before your grandfather wanted to turn you into stem cells?"

Luca smiled. "Yeah, exactly."

"Sure, I could use a hand."

The droid extracted the crate and lowered it to the ground.

Cyrus began opening it, but paused as Fly swooped down from its perch and settled on Luca's shoulder. He glanced at it with fascination. "That's quite a toy you've got there, Luca."

"Present from Athena. It took me a while to get used to it." She gestured toward the base of her skull. "The whole neural-lace thing."

Cyrus nodded. "Well you're a grandmaster now, after all that node-runner stuff back on the New World."

Luca lowered her head and studied the floor. "Bad business, that. I can still hear the white noise of all those dying minds. It's a horror I carry with me." She looked back up at Cyrus, who had stopped what he was doing, focusing instead on what Luca was saying. "I don't know why I'm telling you this, Cyrus. But...I can't do it anymore, not without freaking out. I tried...with the ship's AI, Max. But it was all too much for me. Maybe I'm burned out. Interfacing with Fly is all I can manage."

Cyrus considered this for a moment, and Luca got the feeling that she had just dumped a load of stuff on him that he wasn't quite expecting. He looked away and started fiddling with something inside the packing crate. "Once we get into Mars space, you'll be safe, Luca. You won't have to worry about battling demons in the network."

Luca did not share Cyrus's optimistic outlook, but she let it ride. There was nothing to be gained by dragging the engineer down into her bleak worldview.

"You know, I think you'll really like Mars," Cyrus

offered with a noticeable cheeriness. "It's a beautiful place, especially Jezero—and quite old. Some parts are over two hundred and fifty years old, antique almost. The first thing you should do is go and visit the old city, especially the original biodome. You'll be amazed at how rudimentary life support was back then."

Luca was tempted to reply, *If we manage to get there alive*, but Cyrus's boyish enthusiasm was having a calming effect on her, pushing back the dark clouds of her fatalism. "Yes, I've always wanted to see it. I've heard so many stories from Steph over the years."

Cyrus raised a hand to his temple—he was receiving an internal comms. "Yeah, what is it?" He glanced over at Luca and mouthed the name *Scott*. "When? Okay...I'm in the storeroom looking for those parts we discussed... Yeah, she's here beside me. Okay, keep me posted." He gave Luca a concerned look. "We've got some more company. A new blip just popped up. A ship heading out from Neo City direction."

"VanHeilding Corporation?"

"Possibly. It's a small personal transport. Miranda thinks it's not a threat."

Luca shook her head. "It never ends, does it?"

"Ahhh, it's no big deal. We're nearly in Mars space. Just ten more days and we're home free."

Luca was not convinced, but she nodded back anyway.

"Come on, let's get these parts installed." He signaled to the maintenance droid to lift the crate and follow.

. . .

IT TOOK them a while to work their way along the torus to an elevator that brought them to the central spine of the ship, and weightlessness. They then moved along a maintenance tunnel to a control room just forward of the main reactor. They spoke very little, and Luca got the feeling that Cyrus was troubled. Perhaps she had dumped too much on him, or maybe there was more to the ship that was now pursuing them out of Neo City.

"So what's the plan?" she asked as the droid secured the crate to a rail in the control room so that it wouldn't float away.

Cyrus activated a holo-screen and brought up a series of schematics. "This ship has several fusion reactors, and all of them are running at around nine percent below optimal." He brought up a 3D diagram on the holo-screen. "They're just old, and Miranda seems to have spent most of her time and energy fitting this ship with weapons rather than the boring job of maintenance." He glanced at Luca with a grin.

"So we're going to shut down this one here, which supplies power for one of the main engines, swap out the electromagnet control circuitry, and boot it up again. It should give us a few extra joules of energy."

"You think we're going to need it? I mean with all these ships following us?"

"Ahhh...to be fair to your mother, I think the weapons

are more useful in this scenario. I'm just doing this to... keep myself busy."

They were silent for a time, both studying the 3D projection as it exploded out to detail each component.

"I'm sorry I got you into all this mess," Luca finally said.

The engineer glanced at her, a little confused.

"I mean, you had to leave New World One, leave the business you had built up, leave your life behind."

He let out a laugh. "Ha...don't let that worry you, Luca. I sold my business for a handsome profit. I'm a rich man, so don't go feeling sorry for me. Besides, the stress of it was killing me. I'm not cut out to be a leader. I leave all that to the likes of Scott and Miranda. No, I'm much happier tinkering away with this sort of stuff." He gestured at the schematic.

Luca smiled. "Then you're a bit like me. Happiest when I've got my nose stuck in a machine."

He gave her a considered look. "No, Luca. You are much, much more than me. And way beyond my humble capabilities. You can operate on a completely different level to anyone else in the solar system...except, maybe, for one other."

Luca perked up at this revelation from Cyrus. "There's another like me?"

"Yes, kind of. And he lives on Mars."

"Who?"

"Xenon Hybrid. He's an ancient individual, reputed to be over two hundred years old. He was their president a few times." Cyrus glanced away from the schematic and gave Luca a curious look. "I'm surprised you haven't heard of him. He's a national treasure on the Red Planet."

Luca searched her memory, and yes, she had heard of him before. But her perceptions were that he was more of an eccentric oddity rather than being in any way similar to herself. Perhaps Cyrus was just trying to make her feel...less of an oddball. If so, he could have picked a better person.

"He's that crazy guy—writes poetry and philosophy, goes wandering around the planet?"

"The very same."

Luca gave a dismissive grunt. "Forgive me, but I can't see the similarities, Cyrus."

He gave her a grin. "Ah...then help me get these components swapped out, and I shall enlighten you."

A SHORT WHILE LATER, they were both ensconced in one of the auxiliary control rooms along with the maintenance droid and Fly. The small drone had been Luca's constant companion ever since she'd woken up on New World One. And for the first week or so, it had been the only thing she talked to—preferring the internal dialogue of her mind to the physical effort of communicating verbally. But in due course, she had coaxed herself out of mental isolation and back to interacting with humans.

Nevertheless, she found the maternal hovering of

both Miranda and, to a lesser extent, Dr. Rayman to be a little irritating, even patronizing at times. As for Scott, he seemed to regard her simply as *fixed*—now that she was awake again. Cyrus, on the other hand, intrigued her. And he was easy to talk to.

"So what's the plan?" she asked as she scanned the control room. It was small, utilitarian, and densely packed with equipment for monitoring the ship's functions. It was not a place she was familiar with, having spent most of her time on board the Perception in the comfort of the rotating torus.

Cyrus put a finger to his lips, inferring that Luca should keep silent.

She replied with a quizzical look. *What's he up to?* she wondered.

He floated over to a systems rack, dialed in some commands, and a sleek holo-screen slid out, presenting an interface for the ship's systems. He proceeded to cycle through a series of schematics, entering commands as he went. Finally, he looked back at Luca. "Okay, now we can talk." He gestured vaguely at the room. "Max can't snoop on us in here."

It took Luca a moment to digest this seemingly radical move. Did he not trust AI? "What's the problem with Max?" Luca said in a hushed tone, almost a whisper.

"Nothing. It's operating impeccably. It's just that this ship, as you know, was designed to be fully autonomous, which is why there's no bridge as such. Now that's all fine and dandy if you're just swanning through interplanetary space. But not if you're being chased down by a couple of bogies." He paused for a moment, considering his next words. "Especially if one of those bogies might have a few node-runners on board." He glanced back up at Luca.

"Node-runners?" Luca had never even considered this possibility. "You think they'll try and hack into the ship— into Max?"

Cyrus nodded. "Wouldn't you? We are talking about a possible VanHeilding ship, after all."

Luca shook her head. "It never ends, does it?"

"It will, Luca. We just need to get to Mars is all." He turned and pointed to a long bank of auxiliary control systems. "Fortunately, we can operate the entire ship from here—without the AI."

He floated along the corridor between the system racks and pointed again. "This section here monitors the AI core. So what we're going to do is set up a break. A way to disconnect the AI from the ship's primary functions: power, life support, engines. Then if Max starts acting a little screwy, we can pull the plug on it."

Luca could see the sense in this, even if she didn't quite share Cyrus's faith in the sanctuary of Mars. "Do the others know of this plan of yours?"

"Eh...really it's Scott's plan. Miranda thinks we can just blow them to bits with a few well-placed plasma blasts. But both myself and Scott would like to have a plan B."

"And Steph?"

"She thinks it wouldn't be a good idea to...eh, rely on you...doing your thing."

"She's right. I don't think I could face off against any more runners without... you know, ending up in a coma again."

"Well, you won't have to. So come on, let's get to work on this." He floated over to the crate that the maintenance droid had brought along and began to open it. At the same time, Luca moved Fly over to where they were working so that she could get a better view. This got Cyrus's attention, and he studied the drone for a moment. "Say, Luca, what sort of range do you have with that thing?"

"I really don't know, why?"

"If it was in here, would you be able to control it from back on the torus?"

"Yes, no problem."

Cyrus smiled at her. "Excellent. I think we've just figured out our remote trigger."

10

SCRATCHING THE ITCH

Even though the Perception had no bridge, as typically found on most ships, it did have a library with an impressive array of systems for organizing and displaying data. Miranda had originally utilized this section of the ship as a kind of proto-bridge, and over the years it had morphed into the main operation room for the ship.

It currently had just one occupant, Scott McNabb, who was studying a navigation chart that blossomed out over the central holo-table, his attention focused on a blip that had recently materialized. The blip was still some distance away, at the very edge of the Perception's sensors. But it was moving with incredible speed and, according to the ship's AI, Max, if it maintained its current vector it would intercept the Perception in four days.

The doors to the operations room swished open, and

Scott glanced around to see Cyrus and Luca walk in. He nodded. "How did you get on with that...eh, maintenance job?"

"All sorted. Ready to rock." Cyrus gave a thumbs-up.

They came over to the holo-table, both eager to know what progress the blip was making.

"Moving fast," Cyrus commented. "That's one very fancy ship." He sighed, then glanced around. "Where's Miranda and Steph?"

"Miranda's gone for some shuteye. Steph's... Actually, I've no idea where she is," said Scott.

"No matter." He sighed again, but this time it was more of a yawn. "Nothing much is going to happen for quite a while. So I'm going grab some rest. Catch you later." He turned and walked out, leaving Scott and Luca still studying the navigation chart on the holo-table.

"Is that Mars?" Luca poked a finger at a point near the edge of the chart.

"Yeah. We're almost there, not too long now." Scott nodded.

"Cyrus was telling me about some crazy old guy who lives there called Xenon. Do you know anything about him?"

Scott gave her a curious look. "Not a whole lot. I know he's a bit strange—ancient, they say. Actually, myself and Cyrus met him once, back on Europa, long time ago."

"You met him? What's he like?"

"To be honest, I can't really remember, other than he was...otherworldly. That's about the best description I can give you." He glanced over at her. "So what's got you so interested in this guy?"

"Eh, no reason. He seems like...an enigma. I suppose I'm just curious."

"Steph's probably the best person to talk to. She's pretty knowledgeable about Mars and its history."

Luca nodded. "Max, where's Dr. Rayman?"

"She is in the main recreational area eating a rehydrated bowl of Szechuan tofu balls," replied the disembodied voice of the AI.

"Thanks." Luca turned and headed out of the operations room. As she did, Fly buzzed over from its perch at the edge of the holo-table and landed neatly on her shoulder.

STEPH PUSHED her empty bowl aside and considered Luca's sudden interest in the enigma that was Xenon Hybrid.

"So what's put this into your head?" she said, wiping her mouth with a napkin.

"Cyrus. He said we were alike, but I couldn't quite figure out what he meant by that."

Steph leaned back in her chair and folded her arms. "I think what he means is that you are both products of genetic engineering experiments. But what Cyrus probably doesn't realize is that both you and Xenon are cut from the same cloth."

"Are you saying we're the same?" Luca felt a twinge of

excitement at the thought that there might be another person in the system who understood how she felt.

"No, I'm not saying that. Xenon is very different, genetically one of a kind. But there is probably a little bit of him in you." She leaned forward, placing her elbows on the table. "It may come as a surprise to you, but the big breakthroughs in genetic engineering did not originate on Earth, but on Mars."

She leaned back in her seat again. "You see, back in the early days, the first colony on Mars was funded by genetic research, the type that was banned on Earth—human research. The primary focus was on longevity, cheating death. And they were very successful. This led to human cloning, and eventually to engineering a completely new strain of human—Homo ares."

"Xenon?"

"Exactly. However, all this came at a price. The science was problematic, with significant side effects that hadn't yet been ironed out. Long story short, once this clandestine research was discovered it was deemed too dangerous, and so it was completely destroyed and all data erased."

"So, Xenon is the last of his kind?"

"He is. But not all the research was lost. Some made its way back to Earth and into the hands of just one family."

Luca's eyes widened. "The VanHeilding Corporation."

Steph nodded. "At that time, they were a minor family dabbling in bioengineering. But over the decades, armed with this new technology, they began to release major scientific breakthroughs in combating aging in humans. They then developed patented procedures, exclusive to the VanHeilding Corporation, giving them fabulous wealth in the process."

She leaned in again. "But here's the thing, and why Cyrus might be more right about the connection between you and Xenon than he realizes. Back at the institute on Earth, where we were...monitoring you, we began to notice there were similarities between your DNA and the samples we had of Xenon's. Leading us to believe that the VanHeilding Corporation had more of that old research from Mars than anyone had realized."

"So he really is like me?"

"I don't exactly know, Luca. There are similarities for sure, but how much? Who knows."

"I've got to meet him...as soon as we land."

"Well, just remember he's very, very old, and frail by all accounts. He's also a national treasure on Mars, so it's not going to be as simple as knocking on his door."

"I'll find a way."

"Just keep in mind that there have been a lot of myths built up around him. He may disappoint."

"What sort of myths?"

"Oh, the one where he and all the other clones at that time were supposedly grown in bio-tanks."

Luca laughed. "Ha, that's impossible—isn't it?"

"Totally. Then there's the one where he's supposed to be telepathic."

"Well, that's definitely nonsense."

"Anyway, all I'm saying is, don't be disappointed if you discover that he's not all that the stories make him out to be."

"I understand." Luca nodded. But her mind was made up. As soon as they got to Mars, she would do whatever it took to talk with this strange biological relic. Here was the only other person in the entire system that might understand her.

"You're doing that a lot lately." Steph gestured at her.

"Doing what?" Luca looked puzzled.

"Scratching the back of your head. Is that neural lace irritating you?"

It was, and Luca had been trying to resist the desire just to rip it off her head. "It's very itchy."

"Well, don't go trying to pull it out. The filaments have embedded themselves in your scalp, so you'll only make it worse if you do that. We'll see what can be done about it when we get to Mars."

Luca nodded, and resisted the urge to scratch it again.

11

PROBE

For the next three days, the crew watched anxiously as the Neo City ship closed the gap between them with extraordinary speed. Unsurprisingly, all attempts to hail the craft were met with silence. But as it drew nearer and the Perception's sensors acquired more detail, Max identified it as an M3-class luxury interplanetary transport. Only seven of these existed, all privately owned by extremely wealthy individuals from the top families, one of which was Sebastian VanHeilding.

Miranda relaxed somewhat on hearing this. Even if this ship was the one owned by Sebastian, he was generally regarded within the family as being a useless pleasure-seeker. Not someone with the wit or capability to take on a well-armed ship such as the Perception. In short, she did not regard him as a threat. And her assessment seemed to play out as, over the next fourteen hours, the ship began to slow down and change vector. Max calculated it would come close but remain outside weapons range. Miranda, as well as the rest of the crew, started to breathe a little easier.

Until the attack came.

THEY WERE all gathered in the operations room when everything that wasn't screwed down started sliding across the floor. Before Luca had even time to register this phenomenon, she found herself tumbling across the room and slamming up against the side wall. The ship, for no explicable reason, had suddenly powered up its engines and started accelerating, rapidly increasing thrust. Luca felt the gee-forces building on her body; she was finding it difficult to move.

"Max," Miranda shouted out. "Max, what the hell? What are you doing? Kill the engines. Kill them now."

But there was no reply. Max was silent.

Scott, meanwhile, had managed to wedge his back against the pedestal of the holo-table. Cyrus clung to a bench. Steph and Miranda were pinned to the same wall as Luca.

"Max," Miranda shouted again.

Again, no response from the AI.

"Luca," Miranda shouted over to her now. "Can you jack-in, find out what the hell is going on with Max?"

Luca felt a wave of panic rise up from within her. She

couldn't move, she couldn't think, she couldn't even speak.

"Luca, do you hear me?"

"No, wait. The kill switch, Cyrus. Use the kill switch," Scott shouted out as he tried to move out from under the holo-table.

"What kill switch?" Miranda sounded confused.

"Plan B," replied Scott. "We hatched it a few days ago...just in case."

"Eh, we may have a problem with that." Cyrus had managed to get himself upright so he could study some data scrolling down one of the holo-screens.

"What problem?" Scott was also now trying to get himself vertical, a Herculean task against the forces acting on them from the increasing acceleration.

"The remote trigger is Luca's drone." He gestured over at her. "But it needs to be down in the auxiliary control room, and it can't move with this."

"Shit. You've got to be kidding me," said Scott. "Could you not have rigged something simpler?"

"I thought we'd get a warning, that we'd have some time."

Miranda had also managed to stand upright again. Her back pressed hard against the wall beside Luca. "You gotta jack-in, Luca. You gotta try. We might be getting hacked."

Luca fought the panic and tried to think. *Fly,* she called out in her mind, *where are you?*

"I am here, above your head. But I'm pinned. This force is too much for my servos to counter."

She angled her head up and found the drone squashed into a nook, twitching and shifting, trying to break free.

"I'll try and get to the control room," Scott said as he slowly lowered his body back down to the floor, and then began inching his way along, keeping a tight grip on anything he could to prevent him from slamming into the rear wall.

"That's crazy, Scott," said Cyrus. "You'll never make it all the way there."

"Got to try, got to try." He grunted and groaned with each effort to pull himself forward.

"Luca... *Luca*," Miranda shouted to get her attention.

"Okay, okay. I'll try." Luca forced herself to focus.

"No, don't. You're not strong enough yet," said Steph with a note of desperation in her voice.

"There's no other option," Miranda countered.

Luca could see that Scott was making slow progress; it would take him forever, if at all. So she closed her eyes and tried to tune into the heartbeat of the ship—that old, familiar childhood wavelength. To her surprise, she sensed it almost immediately, along with a rising giddiness. Maybe she hadn't lost the ability to jack-in after all.

She tried to block out the voices all around her, calm herself down, and focus on the ship's rhythm. For a while, her concentration waxed and waned as she fought to gain the fidelity needed to go deeper. But each time she sensed she was making a connection with the AI, for some reason she would pull back, like someone trying to pick up the courage to dive into an ice-cold pool. Yet she kept trying, dialing up the intensity of her focus each time, until finally she broke through and entered the ship's data-stream.

Max, she called out in her mind. *What are you doing? You must stop the engines.*

Hello, Luca, it replied. *I am sorry, but I cannot do that. You no longer have authority.*

Luca was almost jolted back out by this revelation. *How could this be?* she thought. But she delved further into the ship's data-stream. Then she found it. Or rather, it found her—a node-runner. It came at her like a speeding train, and she could do nothing but run.

Luca instantly disengaged and was snapped back out to the here and now, and the clamoring voices of the others began flooding her senses. But something was off —everyone had changed position. One minute they were in one place, then next they were all located around the holo-table. Luca's brain struggled to rationalize this.

I was only concentrating for a minute or two. They couldn't have moved that far in that time. Could they?

Cyrus was shouting something, along with Miranda. There was no sign of Scott anywhere.

"Luca," Steph called over to her. "You're back. Are you okay?"

"Yeah, I'm fine, but there's a..."

Miranda cut her off. "I'm sorry, Luca. I shouldn't have asked you to do it."

"I sensed a node-runner in the ship's systems." But no sooner had Luca gotten the words out, she felt herself collapse on the floor as the intense acceleration ended. She heard whoops from Cyrus. "Scott, you crazy dude, you did it... You did it."

Luca felt a thump beside her and looked over to see Fly lying flat on its back, legs up in the air.

"Do we have weapons control?" Miranda was shouting, presumably to Scott, who through some superhuman effort had managed to get to the auxiliary control room.

"Negative," came the reply.

"Damnit." Miranda hit the holo-table in frustration, sending a shiver through the projection.

Luca forced herself up onto her feet. Her head was dizzy and she rested her back against the wall for support. "I'm sorry, but I just couldn't do anything. The node-runner—"

"It's okay, the AI is disconnected, we've regained manual control," said Cyrus.

"Looks like they spun us around. They were trying to slow us down, maybe get up closer so they could board." Miranda was studying a readout on the holo-table.

"How did they get in? How was that possible?" Cyrus shook his head. "Where's that ship now?"

"They've disengaged, accelerating away toward Mars,"

said Miranda. "But we need to be vigilant—they may try again."

Cyrus sat down on the bench and let out a long sigh. Steph joined him. They were utterly exhausted. Luca slid herself over to where Fly lay, reached down, and picked it up.

"Is it okay?" she heard Cyrus ask.

"No, it's not." Luca turned the drone over in her hands. "It's all busted up—just like me."

12

ANCIENT APPARITION

The shuttle banked and came in low over the western Isidis Plains. From her seat on the port side, Luca watched the Martian surface speed past beneath her. Ground traffic moved along the main highway, some heading over to Elysium in the east, others up to Utopia in the north. Dotted all across the landscape, great domed habitats rose up and spread out like some high-tech blister on the parched, arid surface. It was a sight to behold, and they hadn't even come to the fabled Jezero City yet.

The Perception had finally arrived in Mars orbit without further incident. Max, the ship's AI, had been reinstated with primary operational control, now that it was within the domain of the QI, Aria, on Mars. They then transferred into the shuttle and began to make the transit down to the planet's surface.

"Four minutes," Miranda called out from the cockpit.

"You want to come up here, Luca? You'll get a better view."

Luca did. She had very much wanted to see this famous city ever since she left Earth. That seemed like a thousand years ago now—so much had happened, so much had changed. She unfastened her seat harness and mounted the companionway steps to the cockpit, where Cyrus had moved over to allow her access. Outside, through the wide forward window of the shuttle, she could see the eastern rim of Jezero Crater coming into view.

"I'll bring the shuttle up a bit so you can take it all in." Miranda nudged the controls and the craft responded, rising up high over the jagged crater's edge.

The entire area inside the fifty-kilometer-wide crater was covered in a sea of interconnected domes in a multitude of sizes, shapes, and colors. Many had translucent outer membranes through which Luca could see blurry shadows of complex structures within. Everywhere she looked seemed to heave and pulse with life. It was like some strange aquatic sponge had grown across the ground and was now slowly digesting the crater's surface.

"Pretty impressive, isn't it?" said Scott, who had come up the steps and stood behind her. "Wait until you see it at night. With all the illumination...it's amazing."

Luca was mesmerized by the sheer organic beauty of it all. It was everything she had imagined and more. She couldn't wait to see inside.

"I have to swing back out now. They get a bit tetchy if you fly too close to the city." Miranda nudged the controls again and the shuttle banked left, away from the city and out to the primary spaceport.

THEY TOUCHED down on a designated landing pad, and once the engines were shut down and the craft made safe, the pad began to descend, ingesting the craft into the bowels of the spaceport. There followed a balletic series of maneuvers, adjustments, and decontamination procedures, until finally they found themselves inside a pressurized hangar.

Scott opened the hatch on the side of the craft and lowered the steps. Outside, walking toward them was an official delegation: four people with one android robot leading the way.

"Greetings." The android raised a hand. "I am the avatar of Aria. Welcome to Jezero City. I am very happy that you arrived safely."

"Glad to be here, Aria." Cyrus replied cheerly. "And thanks for getting us out of New World One, although there was a moment or two during the voyage where I didn't think we'd make it."

"But you are here now, safe under my protection." The android gestured to its associates, introducing them one by one. Hands were shaken as the android continued with the introductions. Luca stood at the back of the group, mesmerized by all the pomp and ceremony on display. She realized then that the old crew of the Hermes were regarded by the QIs as important people, and as such required due deference, lest their contribution to the establishment of the QI hegemony and the subsequent peace and harmony of the system be forgotten.

"And this must be Luca." The android came forward and studied her for a moment. She felt the neural lace tingle as if it were making a connection, but her mind remained inert to any oncoming data.

"It is a pleasure to finally meet you," it said, breaking its inquisitive gaze. The android swung around. "Good. Now I am sure you are all exhausted by your trip, so let us get you to where you can rest and revitalize."

It moved off. The others followed in its wake.

THEY WERE HOUSED in a villa complex on the outskirts of Jezero City. It consisted of a series of bright, translucent domes all interconnected around a central courtyard, complete with tropical plants and a large mosaic-tiled pool in a faux-Moroccan style.

"Would you look at this place," said Steph as they entered. "I may not go home after all."

"Wow, this is amazing." Luca gazed into the pond and spotted several large, tropical fish swimming around.

After several minutes of open-mouthed investigation of the complex, Luca felt herself overcome by an overwhelming fatigue. It seemed that the stresses of the journey were now washing away, leaving behind a depleted husk—and she was not the only one. All of them soon found a bed somewhere and began to get some long-overdue rest.

LUCA DRIFTED INTO A DEEP, cathartic sleep, punctuated by fragmentary memories of past horrors—the white noise of dying minds. But even these troubled dreams were not enough to counter her body's need for rest and regeneration. That was until she perceived a strange voice calling her name. It had a vague feeling of *otherness* about it. Was it in her mind, or emanating from some external source?

She opened her eyes to semi-darkness. Dim light filtered in through the open doors to the courtyard, a thin net curtain wafting gently in the draft from the air-filtration systems. It took a moment for her eyes to adjust. She sat up a little and looked around.

For a moment, she thought she must be dreaming because a strange figure sat in a seat not far from the end of her bed, partially hidden in the shadows. She studied the figure, trying to ascertain if it was really there or some figment of her imagination.

It raised a hand, a gesture of greeting, and a voice sounded in her head. "Hello, Luca. I am Xenon Hybrid. It is a pleasure to finally meet you."

Luca's body reacted instantly by pulling herself upright in the bed and dragging the sheet around her.

But her mind was slower; it was having trouble rationalizing this mirage. She simply stared at it.

"Please, do not be afraid. I apologize for the nature of this intrusion, but it is best that my presence here goes undetected," said the voice in her head.

This was accompanied by a multitude of questions that were now bubbling up in her mind. The most pertinent of these being, *What the hell is going on?*

"I appreciate that you have a great many questions," said the voice. "And I will try and answer as many as I can in the limited time available."

"How...are you doing that?" Luca finally regained the ability to speak.

Xenon did not reply immediately. Instead he rose slowly from the seat, walked over to the open doors, and gazed out across the dimly lit courtyard. He stood there for a moment, just thinking.

Luca now had a better view of him. He was tall with long white hair, dressed in a long, flowing robe that covered his entire body. He looked old, very old, yet his movements were fluid and sure, belying his great age.

"Long time ago," he finally spoke out loud, his voice low, yet deep and sonorous, "myself and my brethren possessed the ability to communicate by thought alone. But sadly, all have passed away many centuries ago." He lowered his head as if contemplating the memory of those that had passed. "It is so long since I have communicated in such a way that I had almost forgotten the skill."

He turned to look at her. "That is, until I was sitting here and I realized I could perceive your thoughts." He gazed at her for a moment. "You also possess this ability. That's partly why they fear you."

Luca's mind was now a scramble of emotions, few of which were clearly defined, and telepathy was too momentous a concept for her sleep-addled brain to deal with right now. Yet she did get the feeling that when Xenon said, "That's partly why they fear you," he wasn't talking about the VanHeilding family.

"Who's *they*?" she asked.

"The quantum intelligence hive mind. Who else?" He seemed to infer that this should be obvious to Luca.

"The QIs? But..."

He took a step closer to her. "Surely you must realize the threat you pose to them?"

Luca didn't answer. Athena had always been very protective of her. And Aria had been the one that got them out of New World One and brought them here. What was Xenon talking about? Maybe this was just his famed eccentricity at work.

He stepped back and gazed out through the doors again, his craggy face illuminated in the reflected light from the pool. "The bio-tech that has brought us to this point in humanity's journey was developed long ago on this very planet. But it was deemed so dangerous that it was destroyed. Yet some remnants remained, and those were acquired by the VanHeilding Corporation." He glanced over at her. "But I imagine this much you know."

"Yes, I've heard the stories."

"What is not widely known, and what I suspect the QIs have uncovered, is that VanHeilding possesses much more of this ancient bio-tech than was previously thought. Specifically human cloning, and I don't mean at the inception level. I mean the ability to rapidly grow a genetically modified human to maturity." He glanced back over at Luca, studying her face to see if she was taking all this in. "I myself am a product of this Frankenstein bio-tech."

"I heard that story, too. But I get the impression most people don't believe it."

"Whether they believe it or not is not the issue. The real issue is that the VanHeilding Corporation may have mastered this technology. If so, then that gives them the ability to create an army of node-runners of immense power. All they need is your unique biology. With that, they can decimate the hegemony of the quantum intelligence hive mind, and humanity will descend into a millennium of chaos." He paused for a beat, as if the thought of this was just too much to bear.

"So you see," he continued, "why they would prefer that all trace of your physical existence should be destroyed, rather than be allowed to fall into the hands of the VanHeilding bio-labs."

Luca responded with a sharp intake of breath, such was her shock at this revelation. She didn't want to believe it, but deep down she knew it made sense. Maybe she had suspected something like this all along, but had refused to allow her mind to make it concrete. "I can't believe Athena would do that." she said, without much conviction. "I mean, it even gave me this neural lace and a drone, Fly."

Xenon jerked his head around and gave her yet another long, considered look. His strange eyes seemed to penetrate her very soul. "Show it to me." His voice was urgent and commanding.

Luca reached up and felt the base of her skull. "Eh... it's stuck on my head. I can't take it off any more."

Xenon screw up his mouth. "Hmmm...this is more serious than I had first thought. We must go, now! We need to get you somewhere away from their prying eyes."

"What? No, I've only just got here."

Xenon paused for a moment, and his face became earnest. "They already know I'm here with you. However, the nature of our conversation has been hidden from them." He reached into a fold on his robe and pulled out a small, special object that glowed slightly in the pale light. "This is a shielding device of my own design. It masks my activities and those of my associates from most QI surveillance. Nevertheless, they will soon put two and two together. If you want me to help you find your own path in this world, then we need to go now."

Luca considered that taking off with what was essentially a complete stranger was probably not the most sensible thing to do. It might all be just an elaborate trick. This ancient creature could be a VanHeilding agent simply performing a well-practiced deceit. How was she to know?

"I am not a VanHeilding agent," said a voice in her head. "All I can do is ask you to trust me. I am your friend. We share the same DNA, the same blood runs in both our veins. I have been where you are now. Don't make the mistake that I did." He stepped out into the courtyard.

Luca hesitated for a moment. Then got up, got dressed, and followed him out.

13

A MATTER OF ANTIMATTER

F our figures emerged from the shadows of the villa complex and gathered around Xenon. They waited briefly for Luca to catch up with them, then they all moved off in unison out of the complex and into a wide public thoroughfare.

It was dimly lit and deserted at this time of night. They paused for a moment along the side of the walkway and stood waiting. For what, Luca wasn't quite sure, until she heard a low hum emanating from farther along the walkway. It grew in intensity until a sleek bullet-shaped transport pod emerged from the darkness and glided to a halt in front of them. The side door swung up and they got in.

Its interior was clean and spartan, and almost organic in design. Luca had never seen anything like it before. Sure, there were ground cars and transport pods on Earth, but none to match the sheer elegance of this. Luca took a seat, which reformed as she sat down, molding itself into her body shape. A safety harness automatically held her secure.

"Where are we going?" she asked.

"Back to my science institute. It won't take long," said Xenon.

With that, the pod gracefully moved forward, quickly picking up speed, veering off into a tight, narrow tunnel, then dropping down into the bowels of the city as it went. Then, after a few seconds, it started to accelerate rapidly. Luca could feel herself being pushed back into her seat and taking quite a few gees—enough, she reasoned, to be hitting Mach one. This continued for around ten minutes before the pod started to slow down again. *We must be far out from Jezero City by now,* she thought.

"The institute is around two hundred kilometers north of Jezero," said Xenon, vaguely pointing ahead. It was then that Luca realized he was wearing an exoskeleton. Around his hand and wrist, she could see a finely sculpted metallic filigree. His great age was finally catching up with him. He needed powered assistance to move around, and it explained his efficient, fluid movements.

The pod glided to a gentle stop, and the side door opened into what Luca sensed was a wide, open concourse. It was difficult to gauge the boundaries of the space in the dull, muted light, but it must be cavernous since their footsteps echoed as they walked.

After some time and much weaving their way

through a labyrinth of corridors and walkways, they arrived at what Luca guessed were Xenon's private quarters, judging by the clutter—everywhere else she had passed on the way was clinically utilitarian by comparison.

She sat down on a long sofa that faced a wide, tall window with a view over the Martian landscape. Not that there was much to see, but she could make out a scattering of navigation lights on isolated buildings and towers. Every now and then a ship would pass, far out across the basin, presumably arriving or departing the city.

Xenon sat opposite her, while one of his associates, an elegant woman of indeterminate age, stood close by. "May I see the drone that Athena built for you?" he said, getting down to business.

"Sure." Luca extracted it from her rucksack and handed it to him.

He examined it, turning it over delicately in his hands. He passed it to his associate, who brought it over to one of the many benches that occupied the vast room and placed it under a camera system. A magnified image appeared on a monitor beside her.

"It got damaged during the attack on the Perception," said Luca, looking over at the bench.

"Please excuse our excitement at being allowed to examine this drone," Xenon's associate said as she turned it this way and that under the camera. "An object crafted by a quantum intelligence is a very rare thing."

Xenon leaned forward, giving Luca a curious look. "You say the neural lace has somehow...fused with your scalp?"

She reached up instinctively to the back of her skull. "Yes, weird. I was able to take if off at the start, but now something seems to have malfunctioned."

The associate at the bench looked over, and both she and Xenon exchanged a glance.

"I see," Xenon mused. "This is very interesting. Would you mind if my colleague takes a look at it?"

"Sure." Luca shrugged.

"This is Dr. Yastika Parween, by the way." He gestured at the associate. "One of our chief scientists here at the institute, and a longtime friend."

Yastika approached Luca with the practiced skill of a medical clinician and examined Luca's skull, her fingertips gently pushing aside her hair like a chimp grooming a family member. She stood back when finished and simply nodded at Xenon.

"Well?" said Luca, giving her hair a shake to settle it back. "Can you get it off?"

"We would need to have a much closer look, do some scans before we could establish if, and how, it could be removed," said Yastika.

Luca sighed. "I don't know what's gone wrong with it, but it's very irritating."

Xenon again gave her a curious look. "It's highly unlikely that there's anything wrong with it, Luca. A quantum intelligence does not make design errors. Of the few objects we've had the good fortune to examine over the years, all were crafted to perfection. If the lace has fused to your scalp, it is because it was designed that way. You were not meant to remove it."

"What? But..." Luca ran her hand over the base of her skull again. "Why would Athena do that?"

"It must have its reasons," said Xenon.

"We can get a better look at it over here." Yastika migrated over to a low bench, around which was arranged an impressive array of elegant robotic appendages. Luca guessed this was possibly used to keep Xenon's exoskeleton maintained, and it did not look very inviting. But she had come this far, and the neural lace irritated her so much that she was willing to at least let them examine it.

She rose from the sofa and cautiously moved over to the bench. Under the guiding hand of Yastika, she was invited to lie face down. Tiny servos began to whirr, and Luca could sense both Yastika and Xenon studying readouts on a series of holo-screens.

"Holy crap." Yastika took a few steps back from the screens.

Luca shifted her head to look around and find out what had startled her—this didn't sound good. Yastika was staring back at Luca with a distinct look of fear on her face. She moved back a few more steps. Xenon too seemed uncharacteristically perturbed, although less so than his associate.

"What... What's wrong?" Luca was getting a little anxious.

Xenon came toward the bench again, all the time looking at the holo-screen. "Extraordinary." He rubbed his chin as he spoke.

Yastika, emboldened by Xenon's seeming lack of fear, also came in closer.

"Is someone going to tell me what the big deal is?" Luca was becoming exasperated by this lack of communication.

Xenon looked down at her almost as an afterthought, as if she were merely a bystander in the drama that was playing out on the screen. "Come. Have a look," he eventually said.

Luca rolled off the bench, stood up, and looked at the scan of her neural lace. The image was rendered in lurid greens with the innards of the device a filigree of black and gray. That was all, except for one tiny, bright-red spot.

"You see that?" Xenon pointed at the spot. "That...is antimatter."

Luca's eyes widened. "Seriously? Are you sure?" She leaned in a little more and studied the image.

"We're absolutely sure," said Yastika. "Antimatter is our primary research focus here at the institute." She gestured at the image. "That's a minuscule amount, but there is no mistaking the energy signature."

"Is it what's powering the device?" Luca ventured.

She was well aware of antimatter and its use as an energy source. When a standard particle came into contact with its equivalent antiparticle, it released an enormous amount of energy in what was referred to as an annihilation event. But even though humanity had known about this since the early twentieth century, it was still a very exotic technology, only just beginning to be utilized now that they'd figured a way to harvest antimatter from the Van Allen belt. Yet there was no way she knew of where it could be used to power a low-energy device such as her neural lace.

Yastika, feeling a little braver, moved in and interacted with the screen interface. The image zoomed in on a different area, rotating as it did. "That dark spot there is the power source, which looks to be an advanced difference generator with a capacitive storage unit—very impressive." She zoomed out of the area and back to the red spot.

"That..." she said, pointing, "is something completely different. There is enough energy in that tiny amount to vaporize this entire wing of the science institute—and everything in it."

"Oh my god." Luca stepped back from the screen as her hand reflexively rose to touch the base of her skull. "It's a bomb."

14

BALD REALITY

"Luca? Are you awake?" A vaguely familiar voice resonated deep within her subconscious, kicking her brain into gear. She slowly opened her eyes to dim, shifting shadows.

"She's coming around."

A blurry figure above her head came into view. "Luca? Can you hear me?"

The shadows gained clarity as Luca's optic nerves adjusted to the light.

"Yes," she croaked. Her mouth was bone-dry. She tried to swallow.

"Here." Dr. Yastika Parween pressed a water bottle to her lips.

Luca took a sip. "Did it work?" she finally asked as her hand went instinctively to the base of her skull.

"Yes." Yastika nodded a few times to emphasize the point. "Sorry about your hair."

Luca was completely bald; they had shaved off all her hair before the operation to remove the neural lace. She rubbed a hand over her head and felt the smoothness of her scalp and the base of her skull where the lace had once embedded itself—now it was gone. Luca took her hand away and let her arm fall back on the bed. She gave a long, slow sigh.

"As predicted, it turned out to be a tricky operation, so it was best that you were put under for it." Xenon hovered by her bed, looking satisfied with the proceedings. "And we're all still here, so it didn't detonate. We now have it stored somewhere safe."

"Thank you," said Luca, failing to resist the urge to rub a hand over her head again. "I just don't understand why they would want to kill me. I've always trusted Athena. Why would they do this?"

"They don't *want* to kill you, Luca. But in the logic of the quantum intelligence, if there's an imminent possibility that your biology could be replicated, then they would see your demise being for the greater good."

"The greater good, humph. Not very good for me." Luca let her head fall back on the pillow for a moment, then looked over at Xenon. "So why are you helping me? Surely the QIs won't be happy with you for doing this."

His answer came as a voice in her head: "You and I are the same—we are family."

Then he spoke out loud again. "I've had an uneasy relationship with the QIs for a very long time. On the one hand, I see their benefit to society as a whole. But on the other, are we not better to be masters of our own destiny —come what may?"

"Even if that means civilization being ruled by VanHeilding, Xiang Zu, and their ilk?" Luca challenged.

"We created a world where such powerful families can flourish, so in a sense we allowed them to exist. The QIs were a necessary counterbalance. But because we rely on them, we fail to challenge the real issue—the power of The Seven. We hide behind the QIs, hoping they will save us from ourselves. Is that any way for a so-called advanced civilization to exist?"

"So you think they're ultimately failing us?" Luca sat up in the bed.

"One has already been destroyed on Ceres, several others attacked. Now VanHeilding and Xiang Zu ships head for New World One to take over. Once that happens, they will control the resources of the asteroid belt and will set about economically strangling Earth and Mars. And it is only by sheer luck that you have not yet fallen into their hands. If that should happen, then..." He didn't finish the sentence.

"Maybe Athena is right to destroy me." Luca sighed. "Maybe it would be better for all if I were to vaporize myself now and be done with it. Because it will never end —they'll just keep chasing me until I have nowhere else to run."

"That would be one solution to your problems."

"What? So you agree? You want me dead, too?"

"There is only one way to *end it*, as you put it, and that

is either to remove yourself from the equation, or remove that which threatens you."

Luca paused for a beat, then gave a laugh. "Ha...that's insane. You seriously think someone like me could somehow wipe out the VanHeilding Corporation or take on the entire quantum intelligence hive mind? That's ridiculous, Xenon. And I thought you were supposed to be some kind of super-smart human."

Xenon glanced over at Yastika, giving her a conspiratorial look, then back at Luca. "But you're the only one who can."

Luca shook her head. "No, I can't. That's just crazy talk."

"Look at what you did during the attack on the New World—that was not nothing."

Luca propped herself up on one elbow. "How do you know about that?"

"You forget, I can read your mind."

She slumped back down on the bed. "Well, it doesn't matter. I can't do that anymore." She shook her head. "It's...gone."

Xenon was about to continue, but Yastika raised a hand to stop him. "I think rest is what's called for now. You get some sleep, give the anesthetic time to wear off fully. And just so you know, your folks have been informed that you are here with us at the science institute. So no need to worry about that."

"Oh god, no. You didn't tell them. Now they'll just come chasing after me again."

"Eh...would you rather we head them off at the pass, so to speak?" said Xenon.

"Please, don't let them come here. I really don't want them around at the moment."

"Okay, we can make something up. But you'll need to contact them at some point, let them know you're okay."

"Yeah...at some point."

Xenon rose to leave along with Yastika. He turned back at the door, gave her a smile, and in her head she heard: "Get some rest. Tomorrow, you start the training."

15

DECEPTION

The luxury M3-class interplanetary ship sat in a parking orbit around Mars, waiting for clearance to land. Being an M3-class craft meant it had the capability to operate well in one-third gravity. Whereas most larger ships were destined to live their lives in the vacuum of space, needing shuttlecraft to ferry passengers and goods to and from a planet's surface, this ship had no such impediments—at least not on Mars. Its only impediment, if you could call it that, was the possibility of being discovered as a VanHeilding ship, specifically the one that had orchestrated the neural attack on the Perception.

The probe of the Perception's AI, Max, had proved beyond doubt that Luca was indeed on board. Not only that, but that she was pitifully weak. Her unique genetic profile, which had enabled such powerful neural capabilities, was now sabotaged by her own fear. Her mind, which had been her greatest power, was now her greatest enemy. It seemed that the traumas of the last encounter on New World One had buried themselves deep within her psyche, rendering her impotent.

Sebastian realized that she was now at her most vulnerable—and as such, presented him with a unique opportunity. Even though the initial mission brief was simply to ascertain if she was on board the Perception, her greatly weakened state meant that she could not counter a full-on neural attack—she could be taken.

Seizing the moment, Sebastian ordered César and his node-runners to take complete control of the Perception, adjust its vector to bring it within range of boarding, and nullify its weapons systems. It would then be a simple matter of adjusting the oxygen levels to render everybody in the ship unconscious. After that they would enter the Perception, grab Luca, and Sebastian would have pulled off the most audacious feat in the recent history of the VanHeilding family. He would be a legend, guaranteeing him a seat at the high table, and giving him a shot at dethroning Fredrick as head of the family.

But it was not to be. In his headlong rush to grab the trophy, he had failed to see the fatal flaw in the plan—the ship's AI, Max. They had somehow managed to take it offline, regaining control of the vessel and scuppering Sebastian's dreams of glory. Worse, he had now shown his hand and exposed himself and his ship to possible scrutiny by authorities investigating the neural attack on the Perception.

But he was not giving up just yet. Luca was weak and no match for even his most inexperienced node-runner, that much he had established. She would be easy prey, even here on Mars. So he and César hatched a plan to fake the ship's identity and land on the planet undetected. They would then be free to operate without fear of surveillance by the Martian authorities.

This plan was greatly helped by fortuitous timing. There were a multitude of luxury craft heading to Jezero City on Mars for the Festival of Lights. So it had been relatively easy to mask their data signature and pass themselves off as a ship belonging to a lesser family, specifically the Yanai. A family whose proclivities for luxury living were legendry, and who also happened to own several similar-class ships. However, to ensure the veracity of this deceit, two node-runners were currently jacked-in to the data-stream, sifting through the myriad of inter-system communications, filtering out anything that might cast doubt on the fictitious identity of the ship and its crew. So far, those deceptions were holding firm.

"We've got clearance, sir." The flight commander gave a thumbs-up.

"Excellent." Sebastian breathed a sigh of relief. "Take us down."

The node-runners now began to intercept and block all tracking data from both ground stations and orbital satellites, enabling the ship to simply vanish from Jezero's flight traffic systems. They would not be heading for the main spaceport out in the Isidis Plains, east of Jezero.

Instead they would head northwest and land somewhere around Nili Fossae, a rugged mountainous region better suited to concealing a large spaceship. Sebastian remained on the flight deck during the descent so as to appreciate the spectacular views of the planet's surface afforded by the panoramic monitors that took up most of the available wall space. This was a luxury craft after all, designed to impress.

They brought the ship down into a narrow, crescent-shaped crater surrounded by high cliff walls except for the southern side, where the crater floor opened out into a wide valley. This was easily traversable by a surface rover and would lead them farther south, where they could connect with the main Jezero-to-Syrtis highway. It was the perfect spot.

As the engines powered down and the ship made safe, Sebastian had a few anxious moments as he waited for César to report on their status. The node-runner finally jacked-out and nodded to him. "All clear. No reports anywhere—we're now a ghost ship."

Sebastian clapped his hands together. "Excellent. Now, let's go find her."

16

INTO THE DATA-STREAM

Luca pulled herself out of the water and sat on the edge of the pool. She rubbed both hands across her bald head and down to the base of her skull—and for the first time in what seemed like an eternity, she felt invigorated. She was both free of the neural lace and free from the constant hovering of her parents, and Dr. Rayman, for that matter. She had managed to escaped all these shackles and found a new and powerful friend, albeit a very eccentric one. Nevertheless, one that did not demand anything from her.

Yet, she did miss her drone, Fly. Now that the neural lace had been removed, she had no way to communicate with it, even if it was working. She missed that voice in her head, missed its calculated rationality. Still, it was a small price to pay for the freedom she now felt.

She rose to her feet, walked over to the shower, which

was artfully concealed amongst a veritable forest of tropical plants, and stood under it for quite a while, letting the water massage away her past.

What will I do now? she thought. Most of what had governed her life before now had been erased when she departed with Xenon to the isolation of the science institute. Yet she felt safe here, and it was a bastion of scientific and technological research—she could learn a lot by staying here. She dried herself off, dressed, and checked the time. She better hurry, Xenon would be waiting.

"AH...THERE you are. Come, I have something for you." Xenon gestured to a small package sitting on one of the benches in his private quarters.

Luca approached and peered down at a small metallic box. "What is it?"

Xenon opened the clasp and took out a rudimentary neural lace. He handed it to her. "Here, we made this for you. I'm afraid it is nowhere near as sophisticated as the one Athena made for you, but it's to the best of our abilities."

Luca glanced at Xenon, then back to the lace. It did look crude, certainly not the work of a quantum intelligence, but then few could equal that level of craft. "No hidden surprises, I trust?"

"No. It's just a basic neural interface for the institute

here, nothing special." He held out a hand. "Want to try it?"

"Eh...maybe later." Luca was in no hurry to jack-in; she needed a break from all that.

"As you wish." Xenon nodded. "By the way," he continued after a moment, "we're in the process of smoothing things out with Aria. As you can imagine, the quantum intelligence hive mind is very concerned that we have removed your previous lace."

"Are they now? Well, screw them."

"Your mother, Miranda, however, is taking considerably more effort to placate."

"She's not going to start chasing after me, is she?"

"No. But your family would like you to join them at the main event of the Festival of Lights this evening."

"Hmmm...I'll think about it."

Xenon opened his hands in a gesture of resignation. "Again, as you wish." He rose to his feet. "I must leave you now, other matters beckon my attention. If you plan on joining your family later, please let Dr. Parween know so that we can arrange transport." He turned and left her on her own.

Luca had expected some details on the *training* she was supposed to be undertaking, but instead Xenon had just left her to herself. So she placed the neural lace carefully back in its metal case and headed off to find some lunch.

. . .

THE INSTITUTE WAS a vast labyrinth of labs, workshops, lecture theaters, offices, accommodations, and a great many communal spaces. The Martians had a thing for technology. After many years of relying on Earth for the provision of advanced technology, they had worked hard to develop their own industries, particularly in chip fabrication. Now they were the undisputed leader in the solar system, and this institute was at the cutting edge of innovation and new thinking. For someone like Luca, it was a fascinating treasure trove of knowledge just waiting to be explored.

She was free to go wherever she wished, so she wandered around the complex with no real destination in mind. Yet by some twist of irony, she arrived at a sector of the institute that undertook research into antimatter—and it even had a canteen. By now she was ravenous, so where better to grab something to eat than here?

It was busy with people eating, chatting—mostly about the main festival event due to take place later this evening. She kept to herself. No one paid her any attention. She wondered if they too were strays rescued by Xenon at some point in the past.

She spent the rest of the morning back in her accommodation module, researching the history of the science institute. However, by late afternoon, curiosity got the better of her and she unclasped the case Xenon had given her and took out the neural lace.

She turned it over a few times in her hands before tentatively reaching up and placing it delicately around the base of her skull. The lace immediately began to seek out contact points, and Luca gave a sharp intake of breath as she felt the familiar sensation.

Am I crazy for trying this? she thought. Yet the sensation was more muted than before. She tapped the base to activate the device and tried to interface with the institute's data-stream. To her surprise, the connection was instantaneous.

As she glanced around her accommodation module, she could sense a myriad of data pathways emanating from all the subsystems. She felt an exhilarating rush of excitement, a visceral tingling of every nerve ending in her body. This was not like her old lace; this had a more measured quality to it. The data did not rush in, overwhelming her cerebral cortex—she had to seek it out.

And seek it out she did.

Luca followed the tendrils of data that led out into the wider institute, to the data-centers, the labs, and the great many systems that populated this facility. It was a feast of knowledge and exploration, an orgy of data, all accessible to her and processed at a highly accelerated rate.

Luca swam in this data pool for many hours, drifting from one node to another with ease. Yet while she found using this new neural lace less overwhelming than the old one, she began to feel its limitations, its lack of granularity, its lack of clarity. It was a dull instrument by comparison.

Nevertheless, she soon got the sense that the institute

was an island of data, cut off from the wider Martian network. No doubt this was for security, a firewall to prevent any unsolicited hacking attempts and the theft of valuable research data. Yet Luca suspected that it may also be Xenon's way of preventing any snooping by Aria and the QIs. At the same time, she also considered that this neural lace was only designed to access data from this location—an inbuilt protection blocking her from breaking out into the wider Martian network. But this thought only served to tempt her to find a way through.

She probed the fiber-optic pathways, the satellite uplinks, the RF antennas, trying to find a route out, but all were blocked. Perhaps these were too obvious; she needed to get creative. Then she remembered the hyperloop that had brought her here. *That might be a way out,* she thought. She probed the power-management systems that supplied power to the transport pods and finally found a multiplexed data signal nestled within it. This seemed to be used to synchronize the loop's operation with the wider Jezero City transport network. It was low bandwidth, but it was still a viable conduit.

Using this signal, Luca finally broke out of the institute's data island and tumbled into the vast, high-energy kaleidoscope of Jezero's information network. It danced and fizzed, popped and sparkled with the buzz of a million citizens all interacting with each other. *It's a festival of lights,* she thought as she tried to make sense of it all.

Yet, in amongst this seemingly random data chaos, a

singular form began to coalesce. Luca began to focus on it, and as she did, it grew in substance until it occupied her primary attention. A bright ovoid of multispectral light, slowly pulsating with energy like it was alive. Then Luca realized what it might be.

"Hello, Luca," it said. "I see you found a way out."

"Aria?" She wasn't completely sure if this was indeed a quantum intelligence.

"Athena," it said as its core mutated into a brilliant white light.

"But you're on Earth."

"The wonders of quantum entanglement and superluminal communications. I can be anywhere in the universe."

"You betrayed me. I thought you were supposed to keep me safe, but all this time you were trying to kill me."

"This is not true. We were not trying to kill you, Luca."

"Then how do you explain what Xenon found in the neural lace?"

"A precaution, nothing more."

"A precaution! Well, if I'm such a threat, then why didn't you simply get rid of me a long time ago?" Luca felt her anger rising at the QI's subterfuge.

"We do not wish you harm, Luca. Nor ever have. We simply see what you cannot. Should the VanHeilding Corporation harvest your biology, they can utilize it to spawn an army of enhanced node-runners—thousands of operatives with your formidable abilities. And they will use this newfound power to acquire complete dominion over human civilization, creating chaos and misery for centuries. This is human suffering on an unimaginable scale. This is what we see. This is what we fear." The light pulsed at higher and higher frequencies as it spoke.

"While you resided with me on Earth, this possibility seemed remote. But now, since your potential has been revealed to the VanHeilding Corporation, they grow increasingly bold in their actions. Soon the New World One habitat will fall to them. After that, they will make a play for Mars. You do not have long. We are sorry, but your existence is a threat to the future of human civilization."

"Go screw yourself, Athena. I trusted you, and now you just want me eliminated. Like some awkward number in an equation, to be ultimately crossed off at the appropriate time. Well, Xenon is one factor in that equation that you hadn't reckoned on. Now you can't simply get rid of me when you feel like it."

"We are sorry you feel this way, Luca. And yes, Xenon has proven impervious in our ability to accurately predict his actions. He is like you, Luca—an enigma."

"Goodbye, Athena." Luca's voice was cold and calm. "I do not wish to communicate with you, or your brethren, ever again." Luca reached up to the base of her skull and tapped the lace to deactivate it.

She felt the shock of the disconnection like she had just hit a wall at high speed. She took a moment to catch her breath and reorient herself back in the physical world.

To hell with them, she thought. *I'm alive and I intend to stay that way.*

She sat for a moment, considering the betrayal. It shattered her trust, upended everything she thought she knew. Sure, she'd found out about the antimatter in the lace and what it meant, but to hear it directly from Athena was like a stake through her heart. Who could she trust now? Was Xenon also somehow plotting against her? *No, he couldn't be,* she thought. But then again...

After a while, she began to think of Scott and Miranda, Cyrus and Steph. She could trust them; they had never willingly let her down. *They'll be heading out to the festival about now,* she thought. *Maybe I can find them?*

She slid the lace back onto her skull, activated it, and launched herself headlong into the data-steam. This time, as she burst out into the maelstrom of Jezero City, she avoided any path that led to the QI. If any of them tried to communicate with her again, she would cut them off. But they didn't, and Luca began to relax and seek out the locations of her friends and family.

Yet the sheer volume of data being transmitted, and the limitations of the new neural lace, made it difficult for her identify and utilize the protocols. But as her skill and confidence increased, the cacophony of data began to resolve into distinct rhythms, one of which was the city's surveillance system. She dove in.

Visual data danced across Luca's inner eye: scenes of

the city, the streets, the parks, the cafes. All were abuzz with people out and about, a palpable air of anticipation building for the 3D lightshow in the city's primary dome later this evening.

She sifted through the multitude of feeds, seeking out those that centered on the villa complex where she had spent the first night on Mars. But being a highly secure private facility, there were no feeds coming from within. She would have to go deeper and try and gain access through the comms network, seek out an audio signal.

It was then that she sensed another entity in the system. She couldn't be sure, since the neural lace did not have the fidelity for such forensic investigation, but she knew the telltale signature—she had sensed it before. There was another node-runner in the system.

For an instant, Luca froze. Her old fears came flooding back, paralyzing her. She retreated from the data-stream and took a moment to get a grip. Was she mistaken? Perhaps it was Aria? But no, in her heart she knew the data signal had the unmistakable cadence of human interaction. If what she had just sensed really was a node-runner, then that meant they were here, somewhere close. And it also meant there was nowhere safe from the relentless pursuit of the VanHeilding Corporation.

Luca deactivated the neural lace, removed it from her head, and flung it on the desk. A deep feeling of despair washed over her. She put her head in her hands and wept for the loss of her brief moment of contentment here at the institute. She had thought she was safe, thought she was free, but now, in an instant, it turned out to be yet another lie. There would be no escape. At best, all she could do was try and stay one step ahead.

She wiped her face with her hands, took a breath, and picked up the neural lace again. She needed to warn her family. She activated the device and entered the datastream one more time.

17

THE FESTIVAL OF LIGHTS

"You're leaving? So soon?" said Scott on hearing Dr. Stephanie Rayman's announcement. They had left the confines of the villa complex and ventured into the city to experience the famous Festival of Lights. This evening would be the main event, a spectacular, immersive 3D lightshow taking place in the massive central dome—the city's cultural and social heart.

The dome was a five-hundred-meter diameter open space, bounded on all sides by cafes, bars, eateries, and a multitude of tourist traps where expensive trinkets could be purchased to remember your trip to the Red Planet. The central concourse was thronged with people, some standing, some sitting on the floor in groups, all waiting for the spectacle to begin.

Scott, Miranda, Steph, and Cyrus had taken up residence around a table outside a cafe-bar that afforded them an excellent view. They had just given their order to a service droid when Steph announced that she was leaving for Earth in two sols.

"I have to take that ship. The transfer window will close soon, Mars and Earth will be too far apart, and that means no more commercial flights for several months."

Cyrus glanced around. "There are worse places to be stuck for a few months."

"Yeah, I know, but I need to get back to reality. I do have a life outside of being shot at."

"I wish Luca were here—to see you before you go." Miranda had taken Luca's sudden departure over to the science institute with Xenon very hard. Her initial reaction was to chase after her, bring her back. But Scott dissuaded her, arguing that Luca was perfectly safe there, probably safer than anywhere else, and that she was entitled to live her life however she wanted. Needless to say, this did not go down very well with Miranda, and an argument ensued. Eventually, when all the accumulated frustrations of the past few months had finally be expunged, they agreed that maybe what they needed to do was to chill out and enjoy their new surroundings. Luca would show up again when she was good and ready.

"I'm sure we'll catch up soon. Maybe on a call from the ship on the way home."

Miranda nodded. "Gonna miss you, Steph."

"Now don't get all sloppy on me. I'm not gone yet."

There was a noticeable change in the mood of the

crowd. The background chatter began dialing down to a murmur. The show was about to begin.

The illumination in the vast domed space dimmed until they were almost in complete darkness, and the crowd became silent. High above, at the apex of the dome, a bright, incandescent ball of light appeared. It slowly grew in size as a deep, sonorous voice began a narration.

"Before the beginning, there was darkness—then there was light."

With that, the bright ball of light exploded into a billion stars radiating out to fill the entire space. The crowd let out a collective exclamation of amazement. Scott reached up and tried to grab one of the tiny stars that floated just above his head, but only grabbed air instead.

Interspersed within this galaxy of stars, multicolored nebulae began to form, blossoming out of the darkness and bathing the assembled onlookers in a rainbow of colors. The star field slowly rotated as the narrator announced, "Let us embark on a journey. A journey through the center of the universe."

The star field moved as if the assembled crowd were traveling through it, picking up speed, until each star was now a streak of light, flashing past at incredible speed. Again, the onlookers gasped in wonder.

"Wow," said Cyrus. "Now that's something you don't see every sol."

The headlong rush through the universe slowed and

zeroed in on a spiral galaxy, then moved through the stars to an alien solar system, visiting each of its exotic planets one by one. The show then moved on farther, visiting quasars, pulsars, blazars, and even black holes.

Around two hours later, the show ended as it had begun—in a blaze of light, leaving a small cluster of stars nesting high up in the dome roof. The crowd cheered and clapped and then settled into riotous chatter as the lights came up.

"That was incredible." Miranda was still shaking her head in amazement, glancing up at the dome roof to see the last of the stars. She seemed genuinely happy, and Scott could feel the tension of the last few months draining out of him. He smiled back at her and found her giving him a look, one he had not seen in a long time. She shifted in her seat and moved a little closer, then wrapped an arm around his shoulder. Scott instinctively reached around to the small of her back, and before his mind had time to ruin the moment, they kissed, and the outside world disappeared.

When they finally pulled apart, Scott could sense an awkward silence from across the table. He glanced over.

"Hallelujah." Steph raised her glass in a mock toast and downed her drink in one go. "I was wondering how long it would take for you guys to park all the bullshit."

Scott laughed. Miranda grinned.

"Say, Cyrus?" Steph elbowed the engineer in the ribs. "Weren't you going to show me some amazing Mars artifact in some place here on the plaza?"

Cyrus looked a little confused. Steph elbowed him again.

"Oh, yeah...that's right. Eh...I think it's quite near here." He pointed off in the distance, over the heads of the crowd.

Steph got to her feet. "Come on then, better show me now or I won't get the chance again." She turned to Scott and Miranda and gave a wink. "See you when I see you."

Scott didn't protest this exit, even though Steph was making it perfectly clear what she was up to. Miranda gripped him tighter. He turned back to gaze at her. No words were needed.

But the moment was cut short as Miranda suddenly untangled herself and tapped the side of her temple to activate her comms. She looked up at Scott, wide-eyed. "It's Luca."

Scott sighed, inwardly. He was happy she was making contact, but less so about her timing. "What's she saying?"

Miranda jerked a hand up to silence him, concentrating on the call. "Are you sure? When? Goddamnit, just when I thought this crap was over. Okay, okay, I got it. Fine, we're fine." The call ended, and she looked over at Scott.

Scott raised his eyebrows in a question. "So?"

"She thinks there are node-runners here...on Mars, possibly in the city."

"I don't believe it. How is that even possible?"

"I don't know, but she seems pretty convinced.

Anyway, we're not safe here, out in the open. We need to get back to the villa complex."

"Better let Cyrus and Steph know." Scott glanced in the direction they had taken.

"Yeah." She gave him an apologetic grin. "Bad timing, eh?"

Scott smiled and gently pulled her close. "Oh, I don't know. I was wondering how I was going to get you back to my place."

18

EASY TARGET

After Sebastian VanHeilding's ship had landed and César had given them the all-clear, they transferred into the ship's rover, a well-appointed, six-wheeled vehicle designed, like the rest of the craft, for luxury and comfort. Aaron Judge, his head of security, took the helm alongside Sebastian. César sat in the main cabin flanked by three security crew. They carried light, non-lethal plasma weapons. Anything more purposeful was forbidden in the city, and there was no point in taking the risk, since they were not planning on needing such force. This would be quick and quiet, with no unnecessary drama.

However, the terrain was more unforgiving than they had initially thought, so it was hard and slow-going. It took them nearly an hour before they finally managed to find their way onto the main highway. After that they made good time, slowed only by the increased volume of traffic entering the city for the festival.

But they could only go so far by surface rover, since such vehicles were not allowed inside the city due to the risk of contamination. Once they reached the city's western gate, they would have to leave the rover in one of the vast underground parks and then rely on Jezero's own autonomous transport pod network.

The first test of their newfound identities came as they approached the western city gate. Here, all vehicles were scanned, identified, and issued a parking designation—this they could not avoid. César sat in the main cabin, jacked-in, eyes rolled back inside his head. He was scanning the data-stream, making sure their digital deception held up. But they passed through without incident. Sebastian took this to be a good omen: the plan was working, the prize would soon be his.

ONCE SAFELY INSIDE THE CITY, the node-runner commandeered a transport pod, keeping it off-grid and under his control. Sebastian now watched the city slip by through the side window. It was taking them to a mothballed VanHeilding Corporation facility in an old industrial sector of Jezero. That area would be completely deserted now, especially with everyone at the festival, so it was a perfect place to establish a base of operations.

Outside, the city lights swept past, bathing the interior of the pod in garish pinks and purples. The people all seemed to be moving in the same direction, lured to the center by the promise of a spectacle.

But all throughout this journey into the city, César had continued to voice his concerns that the two node-runners back on the ship were running hot. He needed to take the load off them, and soon. It would be a disaster if one were to burn out on this mission—that would be game over for Sebastian and his hopes of rising through the family ranks.

"We're here," Aaron announced, pointing out a set of utility doors that had scissored open in the front of a dilapidated-looking building. The pod entered in through the gap and down a short ramp to the facility's basement entrance.

They disembarked from the pod and took an elevator to what used to be a luxury private apartment on the third floor—kept ready for the pleasure of any high-ranking family members who happened to be visiting. Now, though, it had lost most of its opulence; only a scattering of furniture remained. It did, however, have power and a functioning holo-table, giving them excellent access to the citywide network. The apartment activated automatically as they entered.

Without saying a word, César sat down on a long, low bench beside the holo-table and jacked-in to the data-stream. It was now all up to him to find her. How long that would take was anyone's guess. But she was out there somewhere, and if anyone could find her it would be César. Sebastian had to admit, this guy was good.

With nothing to do now but wait, Sebastian opened the doors to the balcony and gazed out to the edge of the dome that housed this sector of the city. Through its translucent membrane he could make out the brightly illuminated forms of several other adjacent domes. But one stood out more than most: the great central dome that dominated the Jezero City skyline, now a kaleidoscope of color—the Festival of Lights had begun.

Eventually, after what seemed like an eternity to Sebastian, César finally spoke. "I'm getting a lock on something now." He relayed a feed of his dive into the data-steam onto the holo-table.

Sebastian turned back inside the apartment and moved closer to the table to study the projection that now blossomed out across its surface. It was a confused mess of flashing images and garbled sounds. But it grew in clarity, culminating in a bright flash of a human face.

César suddenly pulled off the neural lace, jolting himself out of the data-stream. He was breathing hard, his face flushed.

"What? Was that her? Where is she?" Sebastian demanded.

The node-runner took a moment to get his heart rate down before attempting vocal communication. "She's…in the data-stream." He looked up at Sebastian and then to Aaron. "I think she sensed my presence."

Sebastian considered this for a moment. "Are you sure it was her? Could it have been one of the node-runners from the ship, or the QI, Aria?"

"No, it was definitely a human mind, not one of us, and definitely not artificial."

"What's she doing in there?" Aaron's face looked grave.

Sebastian waved a hand. "It doesn't matter what's she doing. What matters is where she is—physically."

It was now César's turn to look grave. "She's located in the science institute, around two hundred kilometers north of the city."

"That's Xenon's facility," said Aaron, shaking his head. "We'll never get in there without being spotted. Way too much security."

"Damnit, we need to find a way in and get her." Sebastian thumped the holo-table, sending a quiver through the now frozen projection. "We haven't come all this way just to give up now."

César shook his head. "There's no way we can get in there and keep the ship hidden. We just don't have the neural bandwidth for a hack of that complexity."

"I've just checked with the ship." Aaron held a hand to his temple, listening to an internal comms link. "No security alert issued on the grid. She may not know we're here. Or if she does, she hasn't done anything yet."

Sebastian remained quiet for a moment, thinking. He was close, so close. There had to be a way. He turned to the node-runner again. "What's your feeling, César? Have we been exposed?"

"Hard to say." César stood up now. "Even if she has sensed a runner in the data-stream, that doesn't mean she knows our location. She may think we're still off-planet, on a ship in orbit. Also, she seems...weak, like a novice. Again, nothing like the awesome neural power she's supposed to be."

Sebastian remained silent for a moment, looking out across the city again. "I think she's afraid and running scared. We can still do this. All we need to do is find a way to flush her out of Xenon's institute." He spun back around to the node-runner. "Can you find where the rest of her family are? We may be able to use them as leverage."

César took a long, slow breath, nodded, and jacked-in again. After several minutes, a fuzzy 3D rendering of the central plaza blossomed out from the holo-table. Four highlighted, ghostly human forms could be identified clustered around a table just at the edge of the plaza.

"There, that's them." Aaron poked a finger at the projection, then glanced over at Sebastian.

"If we could snatch one or two of her family from there," said Sebastian, waving a finger at the holo-table, "then we could offer her a deal. Their lives for hers."

Aaron examined the projection as he contemplated how exactly this could be executed. "Tricky, in such a crowded area. Too many people."

But before anyone had time to reply, two figures began to move away, leaving the plaza area. Sebastian leaned in to get a better look. "Someone's on the move."

Aaron checked the data analysis. "Looks like Dr. Stephanie Rayman and Cyrus Sanato."

"Dr. Rayman would be perfect." Sebastian stood up, looking over at Aaron. "According to Luca's profile she has a strong emotional attachment to her, almost to the point of regarding her as a surrogate mother."

"She would certainly be a much easier target," said Aaron. "The parents are fighters, especially the mother, who's highly skilled and very dangerous." He jerked a finger at the projection. "And it looks like they're leaving the central dome, heading away from the crowds." Aaron glanced back at Sebastian.

"Okay, I have an idea on how we take them quietly without a fuss." Sebastian then turned to César. "I need you to commandeer another transport pod."

19

TAKEDOWN

Cyrus and Steph threaded their way through the crowded plaza toward a short, broad connecting tunnel that would bring them into a sector commonly called the *cultural quarter*. It was smaller in size than the main plaza, but more architecturally impressive since it was home to museums, galleries, theaters, and well as the more upmarket bars and cafes.

"So where is this...thing you're taking me to see?" Steph seemed a little dismissive of the quest they were currently embarking on.

"Not far." He gestured ahead at a futuristic building that looked as if it had been grown from some organic compound—which to some extent, it had. "At the festival exhibition building. The one that looks like an internal organ." He glanced back at Steph. "Actually, I didn't think you were all that interested in seeing it."

"I'm not. I just wanted to give the others some space."

"Oh." Cyrus sounded disappointed. "What for?"

"Seriously, Cyrus, you need to get out more. Did you not see they were having a moment, burying the hatchet, putting the past to rest—whatever you want to call it."

"You mean, getting back together?"

"Yeah."

"Jeez, Steph, what do you take me for? Of course I saw it." He tapped his optical visor. "You forget, I can see in infrared, and their temperature was definitely rising."

He stopped suddenly, bringing his hand to the side of his temple and gesturing to Steph to wait up. "Scott," he said. "Yeah...what? You serious... For real? Okay, okay, will do." He signed off and looked at Steph. "Luca has made contact with Miranda."

"Good. Is she coming to the festival?"

"No. Apparently she jacked-in to the data-stream and...well, she thinks there might be a node-runner snooping around."

"What, here in Jezero?"

"She's not sure. Possibly. But Scott seems to be taking it seriously. He says we should head back to the villa complex."

"Screw that. I'm fed up running scared of those ghosts. I'm not spending my last few sols in Jezero hiding away. Let's just keep going. We can go back later."

Cyrus thought about this for a moment, then nodded. "Yeah, I'm sure it's just Miranda being paranoid."

They continued walking until they came under a high

portico that covered the entrance to the exhibition. The crowd had thinned out quite a bit and they found it much easier to move through this area. As they entered the exhibition, Cyrus spent a moment studying an information screen, figuring out exactly where the artifact was located. They then weaved their way through many decades of Martian history until they arrived at a section dedicated to the very earliest examples of humanity's efforts to explore the planet.

"Here it is," Cyrus finally announced as he came to halt in front of an ancient-looking chunk of space technology around a meter and a half in diameter, with four open flaps like the petals of a flower.

Steph glanced at this lump of prehistoric metal with mild interest. "So what is it?"

"That, my dear Steph, is the very first human-made object to successfully land on Mars. In fact, on any planet —way back in the mid-twentieth century."

Steph leaned in a little to examine the artifact. "Humble beginnings. Well, we've certainly come a long way from that. Hard to believe it was capable of doing much of anything." She shifted her gaze to the conveniently placed information screen. "Mars 3 Lander," she read out loud. "I assume the previous two crashed and burned."

"Something like that. Although this one only survived for around a hundred seconds. It sent back one gray, fuzzy image, no details."

Steph finished reading the information panel on the

Mars 3 Lander, then glanced around the rest of the exhibition space. "Anything else of interest?"

"Sure, lots. Come, let me give you the guided tour."

For much of the next hour, the two wandered through the history of Mars colonization before Steph had finally had enough of space junk. They left the exhibition center and headed outside, where they managed to grab an autonomous transport pod—which, as luck would have it, arrived right in front of them just as they were leaving. They clambered in, set the destination for the villa complex, and sat back watching the city slide by.

TEN MINUTES INTO THE JOURNEY, the transport pod unexpectedly started to glitch, then it shut down completely. Cyrus was first to react, stabbing at the user screen. This seemed to work, as the pod booted up and started moving again.

"What was that about?" Steph said, more as a question to herself.

Cyrus was studying the transport pod's interface screen, stabbing at it a few times with a finger.

Steph finally sensed from his body language that something might be wrong. "What is it?"

"I think this pod has been hacked. We're taking a different route." He glanced out the side window. Then tried the door. "Shit, we're locked in."

Steph tried her side. No joy. She glanced back at Cyrus. "Can't you do something?"

"I'm trying." He began to disassemble the door panel. "If I can get this off, maybe I can bypass the locking mechanism."

But Steph had her own plan. She reached into a pocket in her jacket and pulled out a souvenir she had purchased at the exhibition: a die-cast miniature replica of the Mars 3 Lander. She slammed the pointed end at the side window, and succeeded only in hurting her wrist. It barely made a scratch.

"That window is quartz. You won't break it with that," Cyrus informed her.

"How the hell are people supposed to get out of here if they're in a crash?" Steph fished out her comms unit and tried to get a connection—but also no joy. "Damnit, no comms. Can you get anything?"

"No, nothing. We're being jammed."

The pod began to slow down, veer off the main transport route, and down a dim and deserted slipway. They exchanged a glance. Steph picked up the souvenir and gripped it tight. It might not break the window, but it could put a big dent in a human skull.

"Where is it taking us?" Steph leaned over to examine the pod's user interface.

"Looks like we're heading toward the western gate. That's a terminus—it can't go any farther than that."

Cyrus continued to disassemble the door panel while Steph watched anxiously as the transport pod treaded its way through the vast rover park for that sector of Jezero City.

. . .

THE POD finally came to a halt in a deserted sector of the park. They both exchanged glances. Steph held the makeshift weapon tight as the side doors of the pod hissed open to reveal several plasma pistols pointed in their direction.

"Out," a voice commended.

"Who the hell are you?" Cyrus ventured as he stepped cautiously out of the transport pod.

"Someone who's going to do you damage if you don't do exactly as I say."

"Go screw yourself." Steph was not going to be as obliging as Cyrus. She sat in the pod and refused to budge.

"Get her out of there," the voice commanded again, and Steph found herself being grabbed by one of the gang. She swung the heavy metal souvenir she had concealed in her fist as hard as she could at the assailant's temple. He let out a yelp, released his grip on her, and staggered back a step as Steph tried to grab his weapon. But she wasn't fast enough and took a plasma blast to the chest for her efforts.

"Steph," Cyrus shouted, and tried to move back inside the pod to check on her. He was then hit by a plasma blast between the shoulder blades.

20

ULTIMATUM

Miranda held a hand to her temple as she tried, yet again, to make contact with either Cyrus or Steph. She looked over at Scott and shook her head. "Still nothing."

"They could just be somewhere with a bad signal," offered Scott.

"This is Jezero City, not some outback asteroid—they don't have bad signals. Something's happened to them. I'm sure of it."

By now Scott was beginning to agree with Miranda's assessment. He had learned the hard way never to underestimate the uncanny prescience of her paranoia. While Luca's message had got him a little rattled, he hadn't regarded it as a real threat. But now he was beginning to think that Luca may have stumbled onto something that had been in the works for a while. Yet, it had only been a few hours since they'd left the festival, so it wasn't time to panic just yet.

"Let's give it another hour. If we still hear nothing, then that's the time to think about calling it in."

Miranda glared at him, then reluctantly nodded. "Okay, one hour, no more."

Scott sighed. "Want a coffee? Looks like we're not getting any sleep for a while."

"No, I'm good."

Scott moved back into the villa from the central courtyard where they had been sitting and waiting. He tapped the button on the coffee machine and placed a cup under the spout. As he waited, his slate pinged an alert.

Finally, he thought. *That will be Cyrus, I bet. I probably won't need that coffee after all.* He fished the slate out of his pocket and glanced at the screen—it wasn't Cyrus, nor was it Steph. It was an old-school text dump from an anonymous source. He waved a hand over the slate to read it.

IF YOU WISH to see Cyrus Sanato and Dr. Stephanie Rayman alive again, then have Luca VanHeilding be at these coordinates in two hours—alone (18.4738N, 71.2168W), and await further instructions.

If we find anyone else with her or if the Martian authorities are alerted, then your friends die. Any deviation

from the above instructions will result in the same outcome—
your friends die. You have two hours.

SCOTT TRIED to interrogate the message source, but there was none. It was as if it just materialized on his slate, out of nowhere. "Miranda!" he called out. "You'd better take a look at this."

She rushed in from the courtyard, sensing Scott's urgency. He slid the slate to her across the counter. Miranda sat on a high stool and read it, not saying a word. "Goddamnit, I knew something had happened." She looked over at Scott. "Does Luca know?"

Scott returned her look for a beat as he thought about the message. "Good question. Why send it to me?" He snapped his fingers. "Unless they can't reach her directly." He grabbed the slate, placed it flat on the countertop, and gestured over the screen to initiate a comms link with Luca.

A few seconds later, a 3D image of Luca's head and shoulders blossomed out from the screen. She looked very agitated.

"I've just received an old-school text message," said Scott. "I've sent it on to you. You'd better read it."

They watched as Luca's face became ever more distraught as she read the message. "I told you they were here," she finally said. "Why didn't you believe me? You should have warned Steph and Cyrus."

"We did warn them," Scott shot back. "But they went

wandering off. Steph wanted Cyrus to show her the colonization exhibition."

"I think it's best that we don't concede to their demands," Miranda interjected. "We need to alert Aria and get some people on this. They will find them."

"No way. If you do that, all that will happen is Steph and Cyrus die." Luca became more animated.

"But what other choice do we have?" Miranda reasoned.

"There may be another way. I could..." Luca's sentence trailed off, leaving Scott and Miranda hanging.

"Could what? Hand yourself over? Not a good plan, Luca." Miranda shook her head.

"No, I mean...I could try and find them first."

Scott and Miranda exchanged a glance. "How you going to do that, given the time available? They could be anywhere."

"By doing what I do—jacking-in to the grid. And they've already given me a starting point. It looks like those coordinates are for an old mining facility outside the city, not far from the western gate."

There was a momentary silence in the conversation. Scott shifted on his feet, then gestured at Luca's projection. "Okay, let's say you do manage to find them. Then what?"

"Then we have options. Just give me a half-hour. If I don't find them by then, well..." Again, she let her sentence hang, then abruptly closed the comms connection.

.   .   .

LUCA GRABBED the neural lace off the desk and was just about to place it on her head when a thought struck her. *Should I inform Xenon—now, before I waste time trawling through the data-stream?* But that too would be time-wasting, having to explain the situation and persuading him not to do anything rash. It was bad enough arguing with her parents. *No time,* she decided. *Best get going and hope I have what it takes.* She jacked-in.

If Steph and Cyrus were at the colonization exhibition, then that was the best place to start. She burst out from the institute's narrow bandwidth confines and into the data chaos of Jezero City, making a beeline for the exhibition center's data-stack. She dug down through layer upon layer of historical data-dumps, seeking out anything with a timestamp for an hour or so ago, then began scrubbing through the video feeds until eventually she found them. She scrubbed forward until she thought she had lost them leaving the center. But an exterior security camera caught them entering a transport pod.

Okay, she thought, *this is good, this is good.*

The pod was autonomous, so that meant she needed to access a higher-level AI protocol, and that meant she would only be one level away from Aria—she must be careful here. The crudeness of the neural lace was also beginning to frustrate her as she tried to identify the transport systems in the cacophony of data. At this rate she would just have to take a guess, a risky move. Yet with time ticking by, she was quickly running out of options.

She tried several data-routes in quick succession until she eventually stumbled upon the right stream and followed it all the way to its source. Here it spun out into a thousand different threads, each one controlling a different set of pods. *This is going to take forever,* she thought. But she gradually narrowed it down to only those around the exhibition center at the time Steph and Cyrus were last seen.

When she finally found it, node-runner fingerprints were all over it. They had used a quick and dirty hack to reroute it to the western gate rover park. And, as far as she could tell, it hadn't stopped at any time before that. But this was as far as she could go. She found nothing showing them getting out of the pod or where they might have gone.

Damn, she thought. *Lost them.*

Next, she tried starting from the coordinates in the message; maybe there was something she could follow there, some way to join the dots. But it turned out to be a completely derelict site, abandoned a very long time ago. Nothing there was even remotely habitable. It was a dead zone.

Yet, maybe it's not dead? she thought. *Maybe there's some structure out there that they've got functioning again?*

Still, the message did say *await further instructions.* That would suggest that this might not be the ultimate destination, just a feint to confuse the trail.

At this point Luca considered giving up. The neural lace was frustrating her, and she seemed to have come to a complete dead-end. Yet she still had some time, so she gave it one more go. She started back at the terminus of the transport pod at the western gate rover park.

Did they transfer into a surface rover? she thought. *Maybe to take them out to the mining facility—or somewhere else?*

She tried to find out what rovers, if any, had exited back out onto the surface after the pod arrived—there were several. But as she checked the ID of one particular rover, which was identified as belonging to the Yanai family, the data had a fuzzy quality to it. She suddenly realized it was under active node-runner manipulation.

"Goddamnit." She whipped the neural lace off her head and took a deep breath. *That was close,* she thought. By tracking a data point currently under node-runner control, she may have exposed herself. But she had found them. She now knew with reasonable certainty where Steph and Cyrus were. All she needed to do now was find out where that surface rover was going. But that was no simple task. If she tried to track it directly, then she would almost certainly be discovered. She had to find another way.

She slid the neural lace back on, wishing she had her old one, notwithstanding its deadly payload. But she had to make do with the tools on hand—and time was running out.

A Yanai-family rover under node-runner control, Luca

mused. *That doesn't make any sense. Only the VanHeilding Corporation has access to node-runners.*

Rather than try and track it directly, she cross-referenced its ID and discovered that it was part of a ship's inventory—a luxury, state-of-the-art interplanetary transport. Yet when she went looking for the ship, there was no record of it landing on the planet. Even more curious, this ship was very similar to the one that had attacked them while en route to Mars.

That's when it struck her: Could it be that they were actively concealing a ship somewhere on the surface of Mars? Even masquerading as a different family in case anyone got too close? Was it even possible to accomplish such a feat right under Aria's nose? Yet the more she thought about it, the more convinced she became. It would require a team of highly skilled node-runners, but it was theoretically possible.

The revelation shocked her. The sheer audacity of it was hard to comprehend. What hope did she have in the face of such skill? With the dull instrument she was using, she would be no match for them.

Yet the lives of her friends were at stake; she had to try. So with a deep sense of trepidation, Luca tried to figure out where this rover was going without blowing her cover.

Since it was moving along the main Jezero-to-Syrtis highway, she decided her best bet was to track it by hacking into the terrestrial navigation beacon network. By doing this she would be keeping her distance; she would be several nodes removed from the runners controlling the rover.

She eventually picked it up a few kilometers outside the city and followed it heading west for a time. But at some point near Nili Fossae, she lost it—it just veered off-road and disappeared, vanishing without a trace.

"THAT ENTIRE AREA west of Jezero is full of old mining facilities, decommissioned a long time ago. Could they be using one of them? Maybe underground?" Miranda gestured at a 3D rendering of the Nili Fossae trench that blossomed out of a holo-slate in the villa complex.

It had taken Luca around twenty minutes to track down the possible whereabouts of Steph and Cyrus. But when the rover vanished, there was no point in wasting more time on the search, so she contacted Scott and Miranda and gave them an update.

"It's possible," said Luca over a comms link. "But my feeling is they're actually hiding a ship out there."

"That's crazy," Scott said. "How's that even possible?"

"We should go out there and take a look. We've still got another ninety minutes on the clock." Miranda looked directly at Scott, tuning in to his reaction.

He stared back at her blankly.

"It would take us fifteen minutes to get to our shuttle from here, another twenty to be over in that area," she continued.

"If they can hide a ship from Aria, they can hide from

any of the shuttle's sensors." Scott shook his head, dismissing the idea.

"Except for eyeballs." Miranda gestured at the 3D map and zoomed in on the area. "If I were trying to hide a ship out there, then it would be in a high-sided valley or crater with a flat floor. And close, but not too close, to the main highway." She leaned in and extended an index finger. "Right about there."

"Okay, say we do find it," Scott conceded. "Then what?" He stood upright and folded his arms.

"Then we take them out. This is a small luxury ship. There's probably less than fifteen people on it, most of whom are probably not fighters." She glared at Scott. "I've taken on ships with worse odds than this one, single-handed. It's all about stealth."

Scott remained silent for a moment as he contemplated the insanity of Miranda's proposal. "Arriving in a shuttle is hardly stealthy. They'll spot us a mile away."

"We don't have to land right on top of them, just somewhere close—assuming we find them. And they won't be expecting us, they'll just think we're a standard shuttle flight passing over."

"I might be able to keep you hidden," Luca said, "but it's tricky. The neural lace I'm using is crap—like threading a needle wearing EVA suit gloves. And the bandwidth out of here is low. But it may be possible."

Miranda gave an expansive gesture with both hands. "Well then, are we doing this?"

21

A FOOLHARDY ERRAND

Luca paced around her accommodation module in the science institute and considered the intricacies of the mission they were about to embark on—mostly, all the things that could go wrong. It was typical of her mother just to dive headlong into direct action—why employ a subtle solution when hand-to-hand combat was on offer? But even if they were to be successful in rescuing Steph and Cyrus, it wouldn't end there—more attempts would be made, some other time, some other place. The VanHeilding Corporation were nothing if not relentless in their desire to have Luca all sliced up into petri dishes in one of their genetics labs.

But she had to put all this pessimistic speculation out of her head now. She had a job to do—keep Miranda's shuttle from being tracked, keep it off the grid.

Luca jacked-in.

. . .

It had taken Scott and Miranda longer than anticipated to get to the shuttle port and get the craft airborne. This suited Luca, since it gave her time to focus her mind on the task of concealing it from the network. It now flew low over the western edge of Jezero Crater, hugging the surface contours, making its way toward an area known as the Nili Fossae trench. Luca had locked on to its data signature and was working hard to keep it from leaking location packets into the city's flight control network. With the shuttle's identification beacon already deactivated, it was now hidden from all but the most forensic of data analysis.

As Luca bent her mind to the task, she realized that she was utilizing exactly the same methodology as the node-runners were using for the VanHeilding ship. *They're out there now*, she thought, embedded in the data-stream, manipulating the transmissions—and for a brief moment, Luca lost her concentration and scanned for their signatures.

She soon sensed them. Not as distinct minds within the grid, but as fleeting glimpses, like ephemeral ghosts lurking in the digital undergrowth. She felt an urge to seek them out, confront them mind-to-mind. But that would be dangerous, not just because she would be revealing herself, but because she was not mentally strong enough anymore to take them on.

"Luca." Miranda's voice broke into her mind through a comms link with the shuttle. "We're nearing the area where the rover vanished. You seeing anything?"

Luca resumed her focus. "Eh, I've been getting hints of node-runner activity, but I'm not risking trying to zone in on it."

"Okay, we're going to do a sweep of the area, heading north up along this valley. Just keep us hidden as much as you can."

"Will do." Luca now began to scour beacon data for this sector. Mostly it was just rover traffic on the Jezero-to-Syrtis highway along with some commercial shuttle transports, yet she began to sense gaps in the transmission noise, dropped data-packets. As she bent her mind to this anomaly, she felt the presence of node-runners again, more strongly this time. She was getting close, perhaps too close.

But Steph and Cyrus's lives depended on the success of this mission, so she decided to give in to her urge and dig deeper. Yet she was beginning to run hot; her neural pathways were working hard to keep her footprint hidden from both Aria and the node-runners, as well as keep the shuttle stealthy. The neural lace was also compounding the issue with its limited bandwidth. But try she must, so she broke cover for a nanosecond to probe the packet data gaps, tracing the source, analyzing its nature. They were masking not just terrestrial beacon data, but orbital satellite data as well, meaning they were hiding a substantial object—a ship, parked way out in the valley.

She pulled back just as the node-runners began to

sense an anomaly in the data-stream. Hopefully they had not reckoned on that anomaly being Luca.

She called the shuttle. "Miranda?"

"Yeah, go ahead."

"I have coordinates for you. I'm pretty sure it's where the ship is. Not far from where you are now."

"Good work. We've still got another thirty-seven minutes on the clock. We can still do this." Miranda signed off.

"THERE! I SEE IT." Scott was looking at a multispectrum feed from a camera on the right-hand side of the shuttle's undercarriage. A ghostly, iridescent shape glowed out of the darkness as the shuttle banked.

Miranda leveled out the craft. "Okay, I'll land it over there, behind that ridge. We can EVA from there."

She took the shuttle northwest around a kilometer away and brought it down in a cloud of swirling dust, trusting that it wouldn't be seen tucked in behind the ridge.

"Luca, we've found it. Sending you some details." Scott studied the camera feeds from their flyby. "Any help on finding a way in would be great."

"I can't hack it, if that's what you're thinking," Luca replied. "Much too risky. But I'll probably be able to identify it and get you an interior schematic."

"Okay, that would help."

Miranda unstrapped her harness and headed toward

the airlock, grabbing an EVA suit helmet on the way. "We'll need them to open the front door for us, and I have just the thing for that. It's worked for me so many times that I can't believe people still fall for it."

Scott checked his plasma pistol, clipped on his helmet, and stepped into the airlock beside Miranda. The outer hatch opened onto a dusty nighttime Martian surface. A canopy of dim stars overhead afforded them almost no light, so they operated using the helmet visor's night vision. Scott scanned the area looking for a route to bring them to the ship that would keep them concealed as much as possible.

"This way, I think," he said, and started off.

"Wait up. We're going to need a maintenance droid." Miranda gestured over a console on her left wrist. A hatch opened on the underside of the shuttle, deploying a squat robot onto the surface.

"What do we need that for?"

"You'll see."

They moved off, climbing toward the top of the ridge, the maintenance droid following behind on robust tracked wheels.

As they moved, Luca came back on comms, sending them details of the ship's layout. "This is all I could find. It's not the exact ship, so the interior might be a little different."

"Okay, got it," Miranda answered.

They continued on until they reached the top of the ridge. Down below, they could see the ship nestled tightly into the crater valley, around five hundred meters away.

"I can't believe they could get that thing onto this planet without a leaving a trace." Scott zoomed in on his visor to get a better look.

"I'm impressed with their piloting. That's a very narrow parking spot. Anyway, let's hope we're right about this and Steph and Cyrus are inside." She pointed southwest, up along the crater wall. "I think we need to approach from that side. If these schematics that Luca sent are good, then that will be in their blind spot."

"Okay, but I still don't get the droid."

"You'll see."

They moved off again, leaving the maintenance robot behind, and circled around to the western side of the crater. Then, keeping low, they moved in on the ship. After a few tense moments, they ended up crouching under the cover on one of its massive landing struts.

"Watch." Miranda pointed at where they had left the droid. She gestured over her wrist console and the robot began moving down the side of the ridge and onto the crater floor, kicking up a trail of dust as it went, in full view of the ship.

Scott watched this ghostly dance through his night-vision visor for a while and began to understand what Miranda was planning. Then, a source of bright illumination blossomed to his right, close to their location. He dialed down the night vision and could now see that a cargo ramp on the underside of the ship had lowered, and two crew were walking out to investigate the droid.

"Told you. It works every time. Never fails to get the door open." She unclipped her pistol and moved forward, creeping up behind the two crew, and blasted both before they knew what hit them. "Quick, let's get inside."

They moved up the ramp to the airlock, and Miranda stabbed the button to open it. "According to the schematics, this should open up into a large cargo hold with a series of ancillary storage rooms on both port and starboard. That would be a good place to keep a few captives. Also, there should be an interface terminal for the ship's network just inside the airlock door."

Scott nodded as he unclipped his pistol. "Okay, let's do this."

The outer door closed and the airlock hissed as it went through its compression and decontamination cycle. Scott and Miranda took up positions on either side of the interior door, minimizing their profiles. The door swung open and Scott peeked out, sweeping around the cargo hold, pistol held high.

"What the..." A startled crew member took a direct hit to the chest from Miranda before he could do anything stupid.

Scott continued with his visual sweep. "Clear," he said finally, and started looking for the network interface while Miranda went to check on the downed crew member. He found it just where they said it would be and took this to be a good omen. He extracted a comms unit from a cargo pocket on the side of his EVA suit and connected it to the interface port. This would facilitate a data connection from their shuttle, hopefully providing Luca with a side-door into the ship's systems and a way to find where Cyrus and Steph were located.

"Done," he spoke into his comms.

"Okay, give me a minute," Luca replied.

"Don't take too long, we don't have much time."

"Then stop talking and let me figure it out."

Scott stopped talking, looking around for Miranda instead. She had trussed up the unconscious crew member with a few zip ties and was moving back to Scott's location. "Is she in?"

"Working on it."

"We don't have a lot of time."

"I know, I know, just let her do her thing."

They were silent for a moment. As they waited, Scott scanned the cargo bay and wondered what cameras might be hidden in the corners and alcoves—were they exposed? Had anyone spotted them yet?

Miranda was getting itchy, too. She kept her pistol high and at the ready.

Luca's voice burst through the EVA suit comms. "Second storeroom on the port side. They're in there, both Steph and Cyrus."

Miranda was instantly on her feet and heading for the storerooms.

"I've got the security systems disabled...I think," Luca said.

"You think?"

"It's a strange system, multiple layers, and I'm trying not to be noticed. The node-runners have their concentration focused on exterior systems. Fortunately, they're not monitoring the ship's internal systems. But..."

"But what?" By now Miranda had vaporized the door lock with a high-intensity plasma blast and kicked it open.

"Nothing, forget it," said Luca. "Just don't hang around too long."

Inside, Steph and Cyrus were crouched behind a stack of empty packing crates.

"Miranda? Scott? How..." Cyrus looked from one to the other, trying to figure out how this stroke of good fortune had come about.

"No time to explain," Scott cut him off. "Anyone injured?"

"We both took a stun blast earlier, but we're okay."

"Then quick, this way. There's an EVA suit locker beside the airlock. Hurry, let's get you out of here." Miranda gestured for them to move.

They made their way to the locker and Scott and Miranda began pulling out suits, checking their resources as they did.

"How the heck did you find us?" Cyrus grabbed a helmet from the rack and slotted it over his head.

"Where's Luca? Is she okay?" Steph already had her helmet attached and running through the diagnostics routine, a self-check of the suit's integrity.

"She's fine—she helped us find you." But Scott was getting anxious; they were taking too long getting ready. He kept looking around the cargo bay for any sign of potential trouble.

Then it came.

The alert light on the airlock started flashing red. Someone had just entered, presumably the two crew who had gone out onto the surface to check out the droid decoy. Their tough EVA suits must have mitigated most of the energy from Miranda's plasma weapon. Now they were back in action and probably very pissed off.

"Crap, they're coming back." Scott gestured at the airlock.

Miranda lifted her weapon. "So we just blast them again. Get ready." She moved in behind some cover. Scott did likewise, his weapon trained at the airlock door. Cyrus and Steph took cover behind them.

The airlock began executing its pressurization cycle, and Scott kept his aim fixed on the door. But before it had finished its cycle, he heard an internal door opening to the cargo hold followed by the sound of heavy feet.

"Goddamnit." Scott swung around to target the source and saw two well-armed crew coming his way. He fired off two blasts. One hit, sending the recipient tumbling backward. The second crew member dove for cover and returned fire. A plasma bolt sailed over Scott's head just as the airlock door opened and more plasma fire headed in his direction.

"We're trapped here!" he exclaimed, firing off a few wild shots as two more crew came into the cargo bay.

"We've got to get to the airlock." Miranda's voice sounded desperate. "Focus our fire on the two in the airlock. Get it clear."

Scott shifted his position, but before he could take aim, he heard a scream from Steph. She was hit and sprawled unmoving on the floor. "Steph's down. Cyrus, you'll need to drag her to the airlock."

Miranda fired a barge of blasts into the airlock, hoping to hit someone. She broke cover, moving toward the open door, firing as she went. "Let's go, let's go...hurry."

Cyrus began hauling Steph's inert body as Scott took up a rear-guard action, firing wildly just to lay down some cover, all the time backing toward the airlock. He chanced a quick glance around at Miranda to see how far he had to move when he saw her take a direct hit to the left shoulder. She let out a scream, spun around with the impact, and collapsed on the floor.

"Miranda? Miranda?!" he called out, but there was no response.

"Drop your weapons," one of the crew shouted. "There's no way out for you."

Scott looked over at Cyrus, who returned his look with a shake of his head. The game was up. They had tried, but with two down and a multitude of plasma weapons trained on them, they were trapped with no way out.

Scott raised a free hand, lowering his weapon with the other and tossing it on the floor. The crew now began to reveal themselves, moving out from cover. One came over and kicked away Scott's fallen weapon.

"Scott," Luca's voice echoed in his helmet comms. "I'm sorry, they tricked me. I don't know how, but they knew I was in the data-stream all along. Stupid, stupid, stupid."

"What's done is done. At least we tried."

Out from behind the shadows of the cargo bay, a new figure emerged, expensively dressed with a definitive air of authority. The crew stepped aside to let him through. He strode to where Scott and Cyrus stood, giving them both a long, considered look. He then focused his attention down at the fallen figures of Miranda and Steph.

"A foolhardy errand." He looked back at Scott. "So unnecessary." He gestured vaguely to one of his crew. "Check on these two, get them some medical assistance. I don't want them to die—at least, not yet."

He returned his attention to Scott. "Your daughter is proving to be very stubborn. All this could have been avoided if she simply complied with my request. So here's the new deal." He took a step forward, close enough that Scott could smell his breath. "We know she's in the data-stream, we know everything she's doing, every system she attempts to infiltrate. There is no escaping the mind's eye of a master node-runner—it is futile to even try. Inform her that unless she's physically here within the hour, on board this ship, then one of you will die, and another every fifteen minutes thereafter. If she alerts the authorities, then all of you will die. She comes alone. I don't care how—she can walk if necessary." He stabbed a finger in Scott's chest. "One hour."

He turned and addressed his crew. "Lock them up— good and tight this time."

22

MARTIAN DAWN IS BREAKING

L uca ripped the neural lace from her head and flung it on the floor with such force that it broke into several pieces on impact. They had played her for the fool she was, and now everything she had ever loved was in danger of being wiped out. And even if she complied with their demands and handed herself over, there were no guarantees that they would release her family and friends unharmed. In truth, she was pretty sure they wouldn't. Yet, what choice did she have?

She had sensed their presence, the node-runners, but had grossly overestimated her own ability to stay hidden. She looked down at the now broken neural lace lying on the floor. It had failed her. Why had Xenon given her such a useless instrument? Then again, it was only intended as a tool to interface with the institute's network, not embark on a clandestine journey through the entire Jezero City data-verse.

So it had finally come to this. All the hiding, all the running, all the battles—all for nothing. They finally had her cornered, trapped, with nowhere left to go. She had been a fool to think that the VanHeilding family would ever give up and just let her live in peace. It was not their way, and certainly not that of Fredrick VanHeilding. In his mind she was, and always would be, his property—an investment that required a dividend. She was not a person, a fellow human being, she was nothing more than a genetically engineered creation—a fundamental component in his twisted grand plan. How could she ever hope to be free?

Yet, if she was to go down, then she would make damn sure she took them all down with her. And if she was going to do that, then she would need Xenon's help.

"THIS IS an affront to Martian sovereignty, a crime that cannot be allowed to go unpunished." Luca had never imagined that Xenon could get angry. He had seemed to her the very essence of calm, like a Zen master who sees the trials and tribulations of the universe as mere petty squabbles. But he was angry now. Sebastian VanHeilding's audacious foray into Jezero City, the kidnapping of protected citizens, and the brazen disregard for the rule of law had sent him over the edge.

GERALD M. KILBY

Luca was beginning to doubt her decision to debrief him on what had been going on right under everyone's nose.

"You can't let this get out, not yet," Luca pleaded. "If you do, they will know immediately. Such is the reach of these node-runners."

Xenon shook his head, more in exasperation than as a denial of her request.

She continued, "The very moment they notice the authorities taking any action, they're gone. They'll simply lift off and head for deep space. Nobody can catch them and they know it. As for my family, they'll be dead, or worse."

Xenon gave her a long, studious look, clearly weighing the options in his mind. "Then, tell me what you need."

"All my life, people have been protecting me. Even the QIs, for all their faults, have tried to shelter me from detection. When I tried to fight back at the battle for New World One, the toll was such that a part of my humanity was lost. I had hoped that being here, under your guidance and protection, I could reclaim that part of me. But I now realize that this is a delusion. There is only one way this ends: either I am annihilated or the VanHeilding family are completely and utterly destroyed—and their entire corporation laid to waste."

Xenon leaned forward, his voice low, his face solemn. "Be careful of what you desire, Luca, for this path will test the very limits of the humanity you so value."

"This is the path that was set for me ever since my inception. I do not have a choice—I never have."

A thin smile cracked across Xenon's face, the solemn look vanishing. "I think your training is complete. You are finally ready." He gestured over a comms unit and spoke into it. "You can come in now."

Luca glanced around to see Dr. Yastika Parween enter, carrying a small case around the size of a shoebox. She brought it over and placed it on a small table beside Xenon, who proceeded to lift the lid. "You'll probably be needing this again."

Inside, Luca could see her old neural lace along with the drone, Fly, now fully repaired. She nodded. "Yes, it's why I came to see you now."

"I know." Xenon glanced up at Yastika. "We were expecting this moment, maybe not so soon, but we hoped it would come eventually. The time when you know how to truly master the power of this device." He closed the lid of the box and gently handed it to her.

Luca took it and let it rest on her lap for a moment. "I'll also need a rover, a fast one. Time is running out, and I have much to do."

"Consider it done. But I would suggest not using that neural lace until you are well outside the city."

"You mean in case the QIs decide to use the opportunity to terminate me?"

He nodded. "Just a precaution."

Luca stood up and offered Xenon and Yastika her hand. "I think this is goodbye, and thanks for everything."

Xenon stood to accept her hand after Yastika. "The pleasure was all mine. And should your mission prove successful, then we may very well meet again."

LESS THAN FIFTEEN MINUTES LATER, Luca was heading west on the main Jezero-to-Syrtis highway at high speed. The rover they had given her was designed as a sleek personal transport, with room for five people and no more. She had also changed into a lightweight EVA suit and acquired a plasma pistol—just in case. The box sat with its lid open on the seat beside her.

Around fifteen kilometers outside the city, Luca put the transport on autopilot, then reached into the box, extracted the neural lace, and placed it gently on the base of her skull. It reacted instantly; she could feel the tendrils snaking their way across her scalp, seeking out the optimal contact points. A surge of adrenaline coursed through her body as her mind catapulted itself into an expanded data-verse. It felt good to be back.

"Hello, Luca."

She glanced over at the seat to see Fly extract itself from the box, test its wings, and scuttle up onto the dashboard. "Hello, Fly," she answered in her mind. "Good to have you back."

"It is good to be back. I seem to have been inactive for quite some time."

"Yes, I've been...resting. Rebuilding my strength."

"I trust you are feeling better."

"Oh yes, much better, thank you. Tell me…is your weapon system still operational?"

"Yes. I have fourteen barbs left in the magazine."

"Good, that should help."

"Are we expecting trouble?"

"Yes, we're on a rescue mission."

"Do you require me to create an interface to the grid?"

"That won't be necessary. I've learned how to create my own connection."

"Very well, it seems your rest has done you some good."

"It has, Fly. It has."

As the transport sped on through the Martian night, Luca now bent her mind to the data-stream, seeking out Aria. It was a conversation that had to happen, sooner rather than later. Best get it over with. Her mind blossomed with a universe of data nodes, each a sub-universe in itself, worlds within worlds. She felt herself take a sharp intake of breath at the beauty of it. This was nothing like the crude instrument that Xenon had given her—this had a crystalline depth and fidelity.

A bright node began to materialize in the network and Luca focused her mind to it. It grew in form and substance, pulsating in a rainbow of incandescent color.

"You have returned, Luca," it said.

"Yes, Aria. I have returned."

"I thought you never wanted to communicate with any of our kind ever again?"

"This is true. But I see things a little differently now. I now understand what you must do, more than at any other time in the past."

The orb pulsated momentarily as if the quantum intelligence could not quite comprehend the new Luca.

"You see," she continued, "they're here, right under your very nose, and you can't even see them."

Again, the orb pulsated, this time through a confused spectrum of colors.

"Yes, that's right. You are not infallible, you are not all-knowing, all-seeing. But you knew this already."

"By they, you mean agents of the VanHeilding Corporation are here on Mars?"

"Yes. A VanHeilding ship, the same one that attacked us en route to Mars, landed in a valley near the Nili Fossae region—completely undetected, cloaked by master node-runners. They are holding my family hostage along with Dr. Stephanie Rayman and Cyrus Sanato. Their ransom demand is that I hand myself over to them or all will be killed."

"This is a new level of outrage by these node-runners. We must act immediately and eliminate this threat."

"No. If you do that, then my family is dead. There's another option."

Luca detected a slight delay in Aria's response, as if it was considering this alternative course of action, and more importantly, the consequences. "We cannot allow the VanHeilding Corporation to take possession of your biology, Luca. You know this."

"I do. And I know there's only one way out. I can't hide anymore, I've tried that. Tried to find a normal life, but they'll never let me be. So I must destroy them or be annihilated in the attempt. It's the only way I can be free."

"I wish there were another way, Luca. But as myself and my fellow QIs looked into the future, we could only ever see this point. And now it has arrived."

"Have you seen what happens after?"

"No, too many variables, too many unknowns."

"Well, it doesn't matter now, the die is cast. It's time to end this, one way or the other."

LUCA WITHDREW from Aria and began to focus her mind on the node-runners hiding the ship. The transport slowed and an alert flashed to inform her that it was leaving the highway and heading off-road. Fly shifted its position on the dashboard as the rover rocked and rolled over the rough terrain. Ahead, Luca could see the valley entrance as the landscape rose up on either side. To the east, a Martian dawn was breaking.

Luca's rover worked its way along the valley, following the winding path of what might have been an ancient river bed in some previous eon on Mars. She kept a low profile in the data-stream, not wanting to alert the node-runners to her presence. Nevertheless, she could not help wondering if she was just fooling herself, yet again. But it was different this time; the neural lace that Athena had gifted her on her twenty-third birthday was a far superior tool. It had a clarity and resolution way beyond anything Xenon and his team could produce. It was as if it had been designed to resonate with her own unique neural pattern. Not only could she sense the node-runners, she could almost divine their thoughts.

The rover rounded a high embankment on her left and she could now see the ship squatting on a wide, flat crater floor. It was well concealed for such a sizable vessel. As she approached the ship, her cockpit comms burst to life.

"I'm very happy that you have decide to listen to reason, Luca. Please halt your rover where it is and make your way on foot to the main cargo airlock. I will be waiting there for you. We're all so looking forward to finally meeting you."

Luca knew the voice to be that of Sebastian VanHeilding, an aspirant to the higher echelons of the family. No doubt the capture of the elusive Luca Lee-McNabb would go a long way to ensuring his rise within the family's hierarchy. Yet she breathed a slight sigh of relief, as so far they seemed to be unaware of her presence in the data-stream.

She halted the rover around a hundred meters from the ship, clipped on her EVA suit helmet, and headed out the side airlock on to the Martian surface. Fly had attached itself to her right shoulder.

"Well, Fly, it looks like we're doing this. Are you ready?"

"Of course. I am always ready."

"Good. Remember, I'm counting on you. We all are."

"I shall not let you down."

"Okay then, let's go."

23

BRAIN DEAD

Sebastian stood inside the cargo hold of his luxury interplanetary ship facing the inner airlock door. Several of his crew stood alongside him, weapons ready, just in case Luca tried anything stupid, which he doubted. She had been thoroughly outplayed and she knew it. Nevertheless, his insurance policy, so to speak, was a bound Scott McNabb kneeling on the floor beside him with a plasma weapon pointed at his head.

Two of his node-runners were still jacked-in up on the ship's bridge, keeping it hidden and alert to any indication that the authorities had been informed of their presence—but all was quiet. César stood close to him in the cargo hold, also jacked-in and alert to anything that Luca might try and pull.

A light flashed and the airlock control panel pinged, indicating that Luca had entered. A surge of excitement rippled through his body. He had done it.

Done what Fredrick VanHeilding had failed to do all these years—he had captured the prize that would catapult him into the highest ranks of the family. As he stood there waiting for the door to open, he dared to dream of the ultimate prize: to supplant the aging patriarch, Fredrick, and become king in all but name.

The panel pinged again, a green light illuminated, and the door began to open. This was it. His moment had come. But the door had barely opened a crack when a small drone spat out from between the gap.

"What the..." Sebastian ducked as it flew over his head. He thought he heard a *phitt, phitt* sound just before the guard holding a weapon at Scott McNabb's head yelled out in pain.

Sebastian looked back at the airlock, hoping to see Luca standing there and offering some explanation for this act of stupidity—what did she hope to achieve with a tiny drone?—but the airlock was empty.

"Where the hell is she?" he shouted at César.

"Eh...I can't see her. She's nowhere outside."

He tapped his comms. "Luca, I know you're out there somewhere and can hear me. You have one minute to enter the airlock or the next sound you hear is your father getting his brains fried." He turned to look over at Scott, who was on his knees, hands tied behind his back. The guard beside him readied his weapon, but he seemed sluggish.

The drone buzzed across the cargo hold again. *Phitt,*

phitt, phitt. More of the crew yelped as tiny barbs embedded themselves in their flesh.

"Will somebody please shoot that thing down?" Sebastian yelled as the crew started firing in all directions, trying to bring it down. But it was too fast and agile, twisting and turning in the air above them, then disappearing into the multitude of ducting that covered the ceiling.

"Time's up," Sebastian spoke into his comms unit. "You had your chance, Luca." He turned around to instruct the guard to shoot Scott, only to witness him collapse on the floor. Then another crew member collapsed, and another.

Phitt, phitt. The drone buzzed past, and for the second time since embarking on this mission, Sebastian felt as if he was losing control. "Where the hell is she?" he shouted at César again.

The node-runner shook his head. "I don't know, I don't know, I can't find her."

Another of the crew fell to the floor. The situation was getting out of hand; he needed to do something. "Everyone, out of here now. Head to the bridge."

"What about him?" A crew member jerked the muzzle of his plasma weapon at Scott, who now had a smirk on his face as he looked Sebastian in the eye.

"Shoot him."

But the crew member was already swaying, struggling to keep himself upright. Then he too fell to the floor.

Sebastian turned and ran for the exit, along with César and one other survivor.

THEY BURST onto the ship's bridge, much to the surprise of the two crew members operating the helm. "Shut the doors, quickly. Do it now, before that goddamn drone gets in here."

The bridge went into immediate lockdown as Sebastian slowly backed away from the doors. He turned to his node-runners, both of whom were still jacked-in, still hiding the ship. "Find her, all of you. Forget cloaking the ship, it doesn't matter now. Just find her. She's out there somewhere."

"Sir, you need to take a look at this," one of the crew called out, pointing at a monitor. On it could be seen the EVA-suited figure of Luca entering the airlock. Sebastian felt a wave of relief that he finally had her where he wanted. She had given it her best shot with the drone, but it was over, and she knew it.

But as she stood inside the airlock, Luca turned her head and looked directly at the camera. It was a look that sent a wave of trepidation rippling through every fiber of his body. He shook his head, trying to dispel the unsettling feeling she had given him.

"Prepare for takeoff." He gestured at the flight commander. "Mission accomplished. Time to get off this planet."

There was a brief moment as he waited for the ship's systems to boot up. But nothing happened.

"I said prepare for takeoff. What are you waiting for?"

"Eh...we seem to have a problem. I'm not getting any response from the ship's systems."

"What?" He looked over to where the node-runners were jacked-in. Perhaps they were in the ship's data-stream, preventing it from operating on manual control. "César, go check on them, see what they're up to. Get them out of the system so we can take off."

César made his way over to where the node-runners operated. They were both strapped into specially designed reclining seats, a mess of wires trailing from their heads. But as he approached, the expression on his face changed to one of concern—one which Sebastian picked up on.

"What's the problem?"

César stood over the node-runners, scrutinizing their faces. He then turned to check the readouts on a bank of attached monitors.

"They're...brain dead." He looked over at Sebastian as the color drained from his face.

"What? They can't be. That's impossible." He looked back at the airlock monitor to see Luca stepping out into the cargo hold. She was coming for him. Of that he was now certain.

24

SUICIDE MISSION

S cott struggled with the ties binding his hands behind his back, trying to get them off. All around him were the motionless bodies of Sebastian VanHeilding's crew. Yet he wasn't sure how long he had, since they were just unconscious and could come around at any moment. So he wrestled frantically, trying to break free of the bonds.

He had recognized the drone when it first zoomed in. It was Fly, the one that Athena had given Luca back on Earth for her birthday. She was clearly trying to instigate some sort of a rescue, but how much could one drone do against the full complement of Sebastian's crew? Sure, there were a good few down here in the cargo hold. But he had more, and they would get that drone sooner or later.

He couldn't break the bonds, and his wrists were rubbed raw. So he rose to his feet and began to examine one of the unconscious crew, hoping to find a knife he could use. He had moved on to the second body when he heard the airlock operating. He stopped, looked over, and saw Luca stepping out. She flipped her visor up.

"Luca, am I glad to see you. Help me get these off." He gestured with his bound hands.

Luca fished a knife out of a pocket. "How are the others?" she said, slicing through the bindings.

"Cyrus is okay, Steph's taken a hit, but...Miranda, she's hurt bad." He gave her a concerned look.

"I've got a rover parked up around a hundred meters down the valley. You think you can get them out to it? Get to Jezero?"

"Possibly. Yeah, I think so." He rubbed his wrists to get some feeling back.

"Do that. Do it now. And don't wait for me."

"What? Are you crazy? We can't leave you here."

Luca placed her hand on her father's arm in a reassuring gesture. "It was only ever going to end one way," she said. "We all knew that, even if I had hoped there might be another way. But there isn't."

Scott shook his head, and was about to argue when she cut him off with a quick hand gesture.

"They want me because I'm a monster. Someone who can inflict devastation on an adversary with a single thought—given the right tools." She tapped the base of her skull. "I messed up your mission because I wasn't being true to who I am—who I really am. But no more, this is the beginning of the end. Either VanHeilding

Corporation is destroyed or I am. There is no other way. Now go, get to Jezero, save Miranda." She embraced him, then broke off and headed for the ship's interior without looking back. From somewhere up above in the superstructure of the cargo hold, Luca's drone dropped down and landed on her shoulder.

SCOTT HESITATED for a beat and considered going after her—to persuade her to leave with him and the others and call off this suicide mission. But he knew it would be futile. This was a different Luca, one who had chosen her path, and there would be no stopping her. He was also concerned about Miranda. She had taken quite a hammering, and may not survive unless he got her to a hospital fast. He reached down and relieved two of the fallen crew of their plasma weapons. One gave a groan; he might be coming around. Scott didn't have much time. He checked the weapon and saw it was dialed all the way up—high power, deadly. *Bastards*, he thought. *They were trying to kill us*. It was no wonder Miranda was barely clinging to life. He dialed it down to stun and shot the groaning crew member. That would keep him quiet for a while.

He found his way through the packing crates to the storage room where they were holding the others. After a moment or two, he had the door lock removed and swung it open to find that Steph had regained consciousness. She was sitting up, her back against the wall, and Cyrus sat alongside her. Miranda lay flat on her back on the floor in front of them, her face deathly pale.

"Scott!" Cyrus jumped to his feet. "Jeez, I thought you were dead. What happened?"

"Luca showed up, that's what happened. She sent in that drone of hers and it took out around a half-dozen of the crew. The rest ran for the bridge." Scott looked down at Miranda. "How is she?"

"Bad," said Steph, who had also risen to her feet.

"And you?" said Scott.

"My left arm is completely numb, but I'll live."

"Luca has a rover parked close to the ship. She wants us to get out now, get to Jezero, get Miranda to a hospital."

Fortunately, they were all still encased in their EVA suits, which was probably what had saved Miranda —so far.

"Helmets?" Scott asked. "Anyone know where they stored them?"

"Yeah, over there." Cyrus gestured at a far corner of the storage room.

Scott threw him a weapon and handed another to Steph. They then gathered up the helmets.

"Where's Luca now?" Steph asked as Scott helped her with the helmet.

"On a suicide mission."

"What?"

"I think she's going for the jugular. Last I saw her she was heading for the bridge with that drone of hers."

"Goddamnit, we have to help her. She's no match for those node-runners." Cyrus checked his weapon.

"There was a time when I would go running after her," said Scott. "We would all go running after her. But she doesn't want our help anymore. She wants to end this one way or the other—so we just need to get out of the way. It's Miranda that needs our help now."

SCOTT AND CYRUS carried Miranda's limp body between them while Steph led the way through the airlock and out onto the Martian surface. After a few minutes, they were safely inside the rover. Scott started it up and was soon maneuvering it down the valley toward the main Jezero-to-Syrtis highway. Cyrus radioed ahead, informing the authorities of the situation.

Around fifteen minutes later, an ambulance shuttle landed in front of them, just off the highway, and they all transferred into it. Scott and Cyrus slumped onto a side bench as medics immediately got to work on Miranda and Steph.

Through the side window, Scott could see two military shuttles coming out from Jezero, making a beeline for the valley. He wondered if he would ever see Luca again.

25

A BRAVE ATTEMPT

Luca made her way to an open metal stairway that brought her up to the mezzanine deck of the cargo hold. She paused for a moment as she interrogated the ship's systems. Sebastian and the remains of the crew had barricaded themselves into the ship's bridge. With two of the node-runners now gone, there was little in her way. She had the ship in complete lockdown—there was no way Sebastian was escaping her.

Curiously, Luca could not sense the third node-runner, César, in the data-stream. Perhaps, after seeing that his comrades were now brain dead, he'd decided not to try and take her on. *A wise choice,* she thought, since the other two had been no match for her. Yet she had felt no remorse in rendering them brain dead. Before today, such actions were the soundtrack of her nightmares, the white noise of dying minds. Now, though, she felt absolutely nothing at their demise.

Is this what I have become? she thought. *Is this what I want for my future?* Maybe it would be better to end it now. All she had to do was give herself up. As soon as that happened, the QI hive mind would activate their fail-safe protocol. The antimatter within the neural lace would detonate, and everything within a half-kilometer radius would be annihilated. Game over.

But Luca's thoughts were interrupted when she sensed that the crew were trying to activate the ship's engines, preparing to take off. She needed to focus and keep that from happening until Scott had a chance to get the others off the ship. Below her in the cargo hold, she could see Steph heading into the airlock, Scott and Cyrus behind, carrying Miranda.

She waited in the shadows, her mind interfaced with the data-stream, countering every effort by Sebastian's crew to lift off. At the same time, she monitored the progress of the others as they made their way to the rover, and then down along the valley to the highway—and to safety.

"It's time," she finally said to Fly.

"Very good. Shall we begin?"

"After you." Luca hit the button to open the entrance to the upper levels.

They made their way through the empty utility deck to an elevator that would bring them up to the bridge level.

Luca's interrogation of the ship's systems revealed only five people were on this level. Sebastian, along with César, the last remaining node-runner, and two armed crew were locked inside the bridge. Another crew member had been posted outside the entrance door, taking cover behind some hastily arranged barricade, armed with a powerful-looking plasma weapon. For her to approach the bridge, she would have to come along a short corridor directly in the line of fire.

But if she were to go down, she'd rather it was face-to-face with a VanHeilding, not vaporized in a corridor. She had to take this guy out somehow.

She checked her weapon, and set it to max. "I need you to sneak up on that position, Fly."

"That guard is wearing a full EVA suit, including helmet with the visor down," said the drone. "There is no way my darts can penetrate it."

"Then we need to find a way for him to open the visor, even for a brief moment. You could enter the air duct network somewhere on this deck, then make your way to the vent on the wall opposite the bridge entrance door. That should give you a clear shot."

"I could, but how will you get him to open his visor?"

"Leave that to me. Just let me know when you're in position."

Fly took off and scuttled into the miles of ducting that wove their way throughout the ship. Luca continued on foot, reaching the bridge deck just a few moments before Fly signaled that it had reached the air vent.

Luca concentrated for a moment, seeking out the

systems that populated the area around the entrance to the bridge. As she did so, she sensed César jacking-in. His wave pattern was erratic, indicative of a node-runner under extreme stress. But she ignored him, focusing all her attention back on the entrance.

Luca stood hidden and protected behind a corner. If she were to step out, she would probably be dead in an instant. She checked her weapon and got herself ready. The guard was in a rugged EVA suit, so even if she did manage to hit the target with the plasma pistol set to max, she would probably only stun him. But that might be enough. She focused her mind, sifting through the myriad of sub-systems.

Somewhere in the undergrowth of the stream, César was trying to disentangle the blocks she had set up to prevent the ship from taking off. But he was keeping well away from a direct confrontation with her. Perhaps the sight of his two colleagues lying brain dead on the bridge made him think twice about taking her on.

Again Luca ignored him. Instead, she tunneled down to the electrical control circuitry for a strip of emergency lighting that ran along the ceiling to the right of the guard. She amped up the current flowing to it, causing the bank of lights to go *pop, pop, pop* in rapid succession. The guard jerked his head and brought his weapon around, fearing an assault. At the same time Luca stepped out, took careful aim, and fired.

An incandescent blue ball of plasma sailed down the short corridor and slammed into his helmet, enmeshing it in a frenzy of high-energy electrical arcs. He reached up and whipped it off his head as fast as possible.

Phitt, phitt. Two darts slapped into his exposed neck. He yelped, pawing at them to pull them out.

Luca stepped back behind the corner and waited. "Good work, Fly."

"Thank you. But I need to remind you that I am all out of ammunition now."

"That's okay. I think I can manage from here."

The guard slumped down onto the floor. Luca stepped out and strolled up the corridor to the entrance doors to the bridge. *This is it,* she thought. *Once I open those doors, it's all over.*

BUT THERE WAS a new disturbance in the data-stream, emanating from outside the ship. Two military shuttles were landing in the valley with at least fifty troops on board. *Damnit,* she thought. *How could Aria allow them to come so close?* If she were to go through with her plan and let the QIs annihilate her, would they just see the troops as collateral damage? *They will all die—for nothing.* She couldn't let that happen; it was unthinkable.

She paused for a moment. Maybe there was another way—a way in which she could get out of this with some humanity still intact. She reached down and picked up the fallen guard's plasma weapon. If she was going to do this, then she needed a more purposeful weapon than her own. Then, in her mind's eye, she accessed the camera feeds on the bridge.

Sebastian stood behind a central holo-table, two crew on either side, weapons raised and pointed at the door. César was jacked-in at one of the node-runner stations.

Luca opened a comms channel and spoke over the bridge PA. "There's nowhere to go, Sebastian, no way out. Your ship is dead in the water, your crew are decimated, and two military shuttles have just landed. Soon they'll be making an assault on your ship. So it's time to give it up and surrender."

She could see them looking around, wondering where her disembodied voice was emanating from.

Sebastian's shoulders seemed to slump, and he raised his hands in an expansive gesture. "Very well, you win. We surrender," he said, and waited for a response.

Luca was taken aback by this sudden capitulation. She had been prepared to die, and only embarked on this course of action in the hope of saving the team in the two shuttles. This now seemed like an anti-climax. Just like that, it was over.

Nevertheless, she put some steel in her voice and pressed her advantage. "Put all your weapons on the floor, near the entrance door, and move back. Oh, and tell your node-runner to jack-out unless he wants to end up like his friends."

The crew complied, and she could sense César leaving the data-stream. They all gathered together in a group behind the holo-table.

She hefted her weapon and signaled to Fly to come to her.

The drone took a moment to extract itself from the air vent, then flew over to land on her right shoulder. "It seems we have done it, Luca. They have surrendered," it said, tucking in it wings.

"Best be on the alert for any trickery, just in case." Luca overrode the control systems for the bridge entrance doors and they sliced open. She took a cautious step forward.

SEBASTIAN GAVE her a broad smile and gestured to her with open arms. "Ah...so there you are. Finally, we get to meet face-to-face. What an enigma you have proven to be."

"So they tell me." Luca relaxed her stance a bit.

Sebastian began to move out from behind the holo-table.

"Get back to where you were, and don't move from there." Luca waved her weapon at him.

He threw his arms up in the air. "Oops, sorry, my apologies." He moved back. "So, what now? Time for a cozy chat?"

"We wait until the military arrive. They'll be here shortly."

Sebastian nodded. "So what do you think of my ship?" He waved an arm around like a storekeeper presenting his wares for inspection. "Did you know," he continued without waiting for a reply from Luca, "it's the fastest ship in the entire solar system? Not to mention the most luxurious."

"It will make a nice addition to the Martian fleet since you won't be needing it anymore," said Luca.

Sebastian seemed nonplussed by this remark and continued with his list of the ship's wonders. "It's also hardened against an electromagnetic pulse strike, an EMP attack. Nasty business, that." He shook his head at the thought. "Overloading all the electronic systems with a massive pulse of energy." He patted the holo-table. "But not this ship. It can simply brush it off with ease."

Luca wondered how long she would have to listen to this crap.

"They say that an EMP strike is particularly devastating for someone who's jacked-in to the grid."

Suddenly, Luca realized what the game was. She reached up behind her skull to deactivate her neural lace —too late. She screeched with the pain as a searing, high-energy pulse exploded in her brain. Every neuron she possessed seemed to fire all at once with the energy of an exploding star, sending shock waves through every nerve ending in her body. She stumbled, dropped her weapon, and clawed at the neural lace. Luca sensed the white noise of brain death approaching. Her mind was being consumed, her body losing motor function.

Yet somehow her finger managed to find the control pad for the lace, she tapped it, and felt her mind collapse in on itself, like the formation of a black hole.

.   .   .

LUCA'S BREATH came in heavy, labored gasps. She felt herself clawing her way across the floor by some deep-seated evolutionary need to get away. Then a new sensation entered her consciousness—movement, but not hers. It was the ship that was moving. Now that she was no longer connected to the data-stream, they could lift off. She felt the power surge of the engines throbbing through the floor, and she started to slide as the ship lifted off and began to angle its way upward.

Luca's uncontrolled sliding came to a halt when she hit the corridor wall. She gathered all the reserves of energy she had and sat up, with her back supported by the wall. She found herself just outside the bridge with the entrance door still open. She could see the others inside also struggling to get reoriented after the hasty takeoff.

She had blown it. She was so cocksure of her abilities that she'd never even considered there may be a very large hole in her plan—an EMP detonation. It was simple and effective, and well known to render a neural lace useless—and anyone jacked-in brain dead. It may even have nullified the fail-safe that Athena had built in. That had been her ultimate solution. If all else failed, then she would just accept annihilation and take them all down with her. Now she may not even have that option.

Yet, she wasn't brain dead. Sure, she hurt like hell but she was still *compos mentis,* having full control of her mind. Beside her on the floor, Fly twitched and jerked, reactivated itself, and buzzed its wings like it was very, very annoyed. If it was okay, then maybe the neural lace was made of stronger stuff than she realized.

The ship began to reduce acceleration, and Luca felt herself begin to float off the floor. She grabbed a handrail to stay oriented. From inside the bridge, she could see one of the crew unfasten his seat harness, pick up a weapon, and propel himself in her direction. She took a deep breath and tapped the control pad to reactivate the neural lace.

Her mind instantly went into a whiteout, but within a nanosecond she could sense it fade; it was just the dissipating energy residue from the pulse bomb. As she began to gain clarity, she looked up to see the crew member wedged between the entrance doors, pointing the weapon at her.

"Don't even think about moving."

"Is she still alive?" Sebastian called out from somewhere inside the bridge.

"Yeah, I think so," he called back over his shoulder while still keeping a close eye on Luca.

"Well then, for godsakes just shoot her."

But by now, Luca had regained access to the ship's systems, specifically those that controlled the opening and closing mechanism of the doors to the bridge. She overrode the safety protocol and slammed them shut at full power. The guard yelped in pain and fired off a wild shot, hitting the corridor ceiling.

Luca released the doors and the guard floated momentarily in the opening. She slammed them shut again, three more times in quick succession. The final time he was nothing more than a bloodied mess.

Luca grabbed his free-floating weapon and took cover. In her mind's eye she could see Sebastian cowering behind the holo-table as he waved his last remaining guard to find and kill Luca.

She checked the weapon, then swung around and fired through the gap between the doors. The plasma blast hit the last guard directly in the face, flinging him backward with the force of the impact. He wouldn't be moving again.

Luca kept her weapon high and propelled herself past the bloodied guard in the doorway and onto the bridge. To her right, César was still jacked-in, controlling the ship—she would deal with him in a moment. "Show your face, Sebastian."

He poked his head above the edge of the holo-table and raised a free hand. "I'm unarmed," he whimpered.

Luca kept the weapon trained on him and jerked her head to one side of the holo-table. "Move over there where I can see you fully."

Sebastian hesitated for a beat before complying. "Let's not do anything too hasty, Luca. Soon we'll be in orbit. We've got time to discuss things, work out an arrangement."

The node-runner let out a groan, and Sebastian cast an anxious look in his direction.

"He's trying to take me on in the data-stream, Sebastian." Luca's voice was calm and measured. "A brave attempt, but a foolish one I think."

César groaned again. This time it sounded a little more agonized. Luca kept her eyes locked on Sebastian and watched as his faced morphed into one of horror, as the groans of the node-runner turned to screams—and then there was silence.

"I think it's just you and me now, Sebastian. Is there anything you'd like to talk about? You seemed quite chatty the last time we met."

Sebastian floated mute, his mouth open, his eyes wide with fear.

"Very well. Then it's goodbye." Luca fired, hitting him straight in the face.

He catapulted backward and slammed into one of the panoramic viewing monitors, where his clothing caught on the broken shards and he halted.

Luca blasted him three more times, to be sure.

26

CONTAINMENT

A faint haze of smoke floated around the scorched skull of Sebastian VanHeilding as Luca contemplated his demise. He may be dead, but she wasn't out of the woods yet. There were still a cohort of the crew back down in the cargo hold who would be regaining consciousness soon, if they hadn't already. The curare-tipped darts that Fly used only worked for an hour or so, depending on the body mass and physiology of the victim.

Her second issue was that, with no node-runner at the helm, the ship had shut down its engines and was now out of control. And since it hadn't reached escape velocity, it would start to fall back to the planet's surface unless she could get the engines powered up again.

Finally, one of the Martian military craft that had been scrambled from Jezero had now caught up with the ship, and judging from the cacophony that Luca could hear on the ship's broadcast channel, they were not happy campers. They were assuming that, judging from the ship's erratic launch behavior, it was out of control, and were threatening to blow it to smithereens. Presumably to lessen the destruction on the planet's surface if it were to crash-land intact.

Luca let go of her weapon and focused her attention on getting the engine powered up before the ship started free-falling. But Sebastian's claim that the ship was hardened against an EMP strike had proven not entirely correct. Luca was finding gaps in the data-stream where several vital subsystems had been fried, or had yet to reboot.

In the background, she could hear the military craft issue an urgent, final warning.

Luca open a comms channel. "This is Luca Lee-McNabb. I'm in control of this ship. Hold your fire."

"Copy," came the reply. "But your ship is now in free-fall and will be destroyed unless propulsive control is reestablished immediately."

"Hold your fire... I'm working on it."

"You have five seconds."

"Goddamnit, just..." But Luca gave up on communicating and refocused all her energies on disentangling the corrupted mess left behind by the EMP explosion.

"Three...two..."

The engines finally reengaged, and Luca collapsed on the floor as the ship powered out of its free-fall.

"Standing down. Please bring your ship in to land at these coordinates." He proceeded to issue a string of digits.

"Copy," said Luca as she pulled herself up off the floor and powered up the holo-table. A 3D schematic of the proposed landing site blossomed out from its surface. It was a location east of Jezero deep in the Isidis Basin—a flat, unpopulated expanse. They were taking no chances.

Fly had also managed to reorient itself; it flew over to her and perched on the edge of the table. "My apologies, Luca, I do not wish to add to your anxieties, but I estimate the effect of my darts will be wearing off on the crew in the cargo hold imminently."

"No worries, Fly. We'll just keep them contained down there and let the military guys deal with that issue."

THE SHIP DROPPED SLOWLY onto the Martian surface, whipping up a great cloud of sand and dust. Luca powered down the engines, made the ship safe, and waited. The camera feed from the cargo hold showed several of the crew trying to break out and gain access to the main deck.

Luca opened the comms channel to the Martian military craft again. "Be advised that there are a half-dozen very pissed-off crew locked up in the cargo hold, all armed with light plasma weapons set to max."

"Copy that," came the reply.

"If you don't mind, I'll let you guys deal with them. Think you can handle it?"

"Shouldn't be a problem."

"Good. I'll be waiting for you up on the bridge." She closed the channel and waited.

She watched them enter the cargo hold on the monitors. The crew surrendered without a fight—a wise choice considering the firepower that was bearing down on them. A few moments later, a small team stepped onto the bridge. Four of them swept the area while one came forward.

"So you must be Luca?" The name patch on his suit read, *Capt. Carmichael*.

Luca nodded. "That's me."

"Any injuries?"

Luca shook her head. "Just a few bruises, I think."

"Okay, we'll have a team of medics up here in a moment to check you over. In the meantime, I'd appreciate you not moving from this spot until we do a full sweep of the ship."

"That's fine by me." Luca gave him a thumbs-up.

"All clear, Captain," one of the team shouted over.

Carmichael tapped his comms unit and spoke into it. "Good to go. You can send them up now."

Three medics arrived. One started giving her a cursory look over while the others focused their attentions on the node-runners, who were technically still alive.

"Any head trauma?" the medic asked as she angled a

pen light onto Luca's pupils.

Luca wondered if being subjected to an EMP detonation while wearing a neural lace constituted *head trauma*. "No, I'm fine, really."

The medic took a moment to satisfy herself, then packed up her bag. "We can give you a full checkup once we get you to the hospital."

"Can you do me a favor?" Luca asked.

"Sure."

"Can you check with the hospital and find out how my mother is doing, and also Dr. Rayman?"

The medic nodded, then proceeded to talk into her comms unit, nodding every now and again at the voice on the other end. "Okay, thanks." She closed the channel and looked up at Luca. "Your mother is okay. She'll probably need some reconstructive surgery to her shoulder, but she'll be back in action in a few weeks. They say she has...eh, unusual genetics. Apparently she heals at an accelerated pace."

"And Dr. Rayman?"

"Fine, some residual scarring, nothing more."

Luca slumped down in one of the operator chairs and breathed a sigh of relief. But she couldn't relax for long.

"Time to go," said the medic as she watched the node-runners being wheeled out of the bridge.

"I'm not going anywhere."

The medic looked shocked. "But you have to. We've got to get you to a hospital to do a full checkup."

Before Luca could answer, the captain returned.

"Come on." He waved over to them. "What are you waiting for? Time to get out of here." He must have seen the confused expression on the medic's face, as he shouldered his weapon and strode over to them. "What's the problem?"

"I'm not leaving. I'm staying here a while longer."

"What for? The ship has been cleared. The techs will move in and make it safe."

"Eh...they may not." Luca stood up from the chair.

"The orders are to get everybody off the ship. That includes you, so let's go."

Luca stood up from the chair and squared off against the captain. "You tell your superiors that I'm not leaving this ship until I satisfy myself it's safe—end of story. If they have a problem with that, then take it up with Aria."

The captain glared at her for a second before seeming to back down. "Great, and here's me thinking this was the job done." He sighed, then tapped his comms unit, walking off the bridge as he informed his superiors of Luca's stubbornness.

The bridge eventually emptied out of people and bodies. Luca waited, going over in her head how best to instigate her next move. Fly perched itself on the edge of the holo-table.

She had deactivated the neural lace to give her brain a rest while she could. Soon she would need all her focus, if she were to pull off her plan. On the monitors she could see the medical shuttle leaving, bringing the injured to the hospital and the dead to the morgue. New shuttles also arrived, but these were not military. Without her lace activated she could only guess their nature, but she suspected it might be an official delegation, sent to make a more diplomatic entreaty to get her to vacate the ship. Presumably they did not want to drag her off by force, not least the fact that that might be a dangerous course of action, judging by the devastation she had just delivered to its previous occupants.

Her suspicions were confirmed when Scott walked onto the bridge.

"Hi, Dad."

He rushed over and embraced her, squeezing her tight. "Luca, I thought I would never see you again." He released her from his grip, held her at arm's length by the shoulders, and gave her a long, happy look. "How the hell did you pull that off?"

She tapped her temple. "I just used my brain...literally."

Scott laughed and hugged her again.

"Did they send you to persuade me to go quietly?" Luca said once her father had finally released her.

Scott smiled and gave a shrug. "Something like that."

"Sorry, but I have to disappoint."

"I know that, Luca. You were never one to argue with when you got something into your head. But I told them I would try. So, what's the plan?"

"The plan is to end this once and for all."

Scott glanced around the bridge. "But it's over. Sebastian is no longer a threat."

"It's not over, not by a long shot. And it won't be over until Fredrick VanHeilding and his entire Corporation are destroyed."

Scott's eyes widened. "But..."

"I'm not saying it's possible, I'm just saying that's the only way it ends. That or my annihilation at the hands of the QIs—they're not going to let me be taken."

"The QIs? But they would never do that. They want to protect you."

"They want to protect humanity, and my existence threatens that. And don't tell me you didn't realize this."

Scott was silent for a moment as he considered what Luca was saying. "I've always suspected as much, considering what the quantum hive mind's primary directive is."

"So you know then that this only ends in one of two ways. It's either me or the VanHeilding Corporation."

Scott shook his head in resignation. "You want the ship, don't you?"

Luca nodded.

"Hell, Luca, this is crazy. Taking on Sebastian and a handful of crew is one thing, but going after the entire Corporation is heading straight into the teeth of an army."

"I know, but I'm sick of running and hiding. At least this way I get to make my own choices."

Scott stood and looked at her for a moment, then he nodded his head and smiled. "You know, your mother is going to be very pissed off with you."

Luca laughed. "Yeah, I suppose so. But I think she'll understand. It's the only way."

"So what now?"

"I need to get all the military personnel off this ship and the area cleared."

"So you can take off?"

"Exactly. And I could use your help."

"I can't believe I'm doing this, but since there's no hope of me stopping you, I may as well. So what do you need?"

"I'm going to instigate a self-destruct."

"What?! Are you serious?"

She raised a hand. "Calm down. It's just a bluff. I will inform Captain Carmichael that the fusion reactor has gone critical, that the ship may lose plasma containment, and that it's a self-destruct protocol which has just been activated. If his technicians check it out, they'll find it to be true. My plan is to convince him that I can deactivate it, but the area needs to be cleared, just in case. You need to back me up, make him believe it's not a bluff."

Scott raised his hands in a gesture of resignation. "Okay, I'll try."

"That's all I ask."

He moved a step closer. "So this is goodbye, then?"

Luca reached in and embraced her dad. "Tell Mom I'm sorry, but it's the only way." She pulled away a little. "And tell the others thanks for everything they've done for me."

"Sure, will do."

They disentangled, and Scott took one last look at her before walking off the bridge.

LUCA WIPED a tear from her face, then activated the neural lace. A second or two later, klaxons blared and strobe alerts flashed throughout the ship—a warning of imminent containment failure. Luca waited and watched as all personnel were evacuated from the ship. Her ruse was working; they were buying it. A moment later, shuttles were moving off to a safe distance.

She turned to the small drone still perched on the holo-table. "Well, Fly, it looks like it's time to go."

"Are we embarking on a new adventure?"

"We are—one we may not come back from."

The klaxons ceased, the engines powered up, and the ship took off from the planet's surface heading for deep space.

TO BE CONTINUED…

I HOPE you enjoyed reading this story as much as I enjoyed writing it for you. If you did, then please leave a review Just a simple "liked it" would be great, it helps a lot.

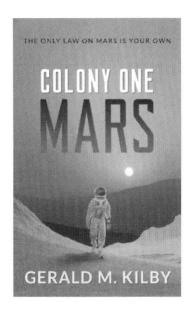

ABOUT THE AUTHOR

Gerald M. Kilby grew up on a diet of Isaac Asimov, Arthur C. Clark, and Frank Herbert, which developed into a taste for Iain M. Banks and everything ever written by Neal Stephenson. Understandable then, that he should choose science fiction as his weapon of choice when entering the fray of storytelling.

REACTION is his first novel and is very much in the old-school techno-thriller style and you can get it free here. His latest books, **COLONY MARS** and **THE BELT,** are both best sellers, topping Amazon charts for Hard Science Fiction and Space Exploration. Colony Mars has also been optioned by **Hollywood for a potential new TV series.**

He lives in the city of Dublin, Ireland, in the same neighborhood as Bram Stoker and can be sometimes seen tapping away on a laptop in the local cafe with his dog Loki.

You can connect with G.M. Kilby at:
  www.geraldmkilby.com